William Shakespeare's Tragical History of Frankenstein

IAN DOESCHER

Based on the novel by Mary Shelley

'Tis alive!

Copyright © 2020 Ian Doescher
All rights reserved.

To Jennifer, again again again.

DRAMATIS PERSONAE

Robert Walton, *explorer and Chorus*

Victor Frankenstein, *a scientist*
The monster, *Victor's creation*
Elizabeth Lavenza, *Victor's adopted cousin and paramour*
Henry Clerval, *Victor's closest friend*
Alphonse Frankenstein, *Victor's father*
Caroline Beaufort Frankenstein, *Victor's mother*
Ernest Frankenstein, *Victor's younger brother*
William Frankenstein, *Victor's youngest brother*
Justine Moritz, *an unfortunate young woman*
De Lacey, *a blind peasant*
Agatha, *De Lacey's daughter*
Felix, *De Lacey's son*
Safie, *Felix's paramour*
Professor Waldman, *Ingolstadt professor of chemistry*
Professor Krempe, *Ingolstadt professor of philosophy*
Kirwin, *a magistrate*

Assorted students, a magistrate, an officer, a clergy person, crew members, villagers, and citizens.

Scene: Europe

WILLIAM SHAKESPEARE'S TRAGICAL HISTORY OF FRANKENSTEIN

Prologue.

Enter ROBERT WALTON as Chorus.

Robert   Fire! Burning fervently within the soul,
Consuming reason, thought, and prudent sense,
Refining passion to a bodkin's edge,
The heat producing sweat from human pores—
Such is the blaze with which I am engulf'd!   5
The flames of orange, blue, red, yellow, white:
A rainbow panoply of fierce desire.
O, what can stop the pure, determin'd heart,
Or snuff out the resolvèd will of man?
My will's bright embers fix'd my compass north,   10
Toward the vast, unconquer'd lands of ice.
Infernal fever for the frozen fields,
Which fann'd my spirit to its singeing point,
Led me to ship, to water, to a trek—
Th'elusive north pole waiting at its end.   15
My scorching ardor for the voyage there
Had burn'd within me constantly for years,
Until, at last, the shipmates were secur'd,
Supplies and sustenance obtain'd in bulk,
And swiftly launch'd our vessel on its way.   20
The trip's commencement smother'd not my fire,
But—like a spark that in a woodland drops,
Which sets a forest whole to raging flames—
My hot desire extended to my crew.
For weeks, we were a band together burnt,   25
Adventure was the flare that lit our route.
It happen'd, on the journey, that our ship
Was caught within the ice floe fixedly.
There, as a candle 'neath a glass will be
Extinguish'd, did my doubts at first arise.   30
Was all the smoldering within our chests

To come to naught? The thought made me afeard.
Soon, though, I did my present fears forget,
For we espied a figure on the ice,
A man approaching through the wilderness.   35
His story 'tis that ye must hear today—
The tragic man whose fire surpass'd e'en mine,
Whose mind was touch'd by true Promethean heat.
If you would venture whither fervor leads,
If you would see a torrid, sordid tale,   40
If you would witness hellfire most malign,
Behold this tale of Victor Frankenstein.

[Exit.

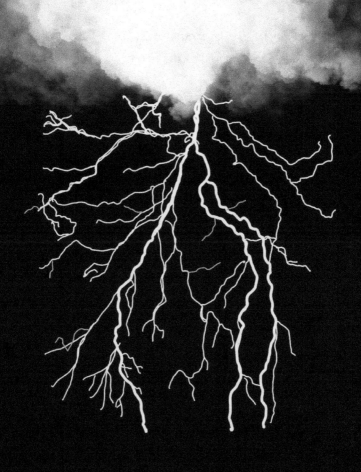

WILLIAM SHAKESPEARE'S TRAGICAL HISTORY OF FRANKENSTEIN

SCENE 1.

Geneva. The Frankenstein household.

Enter VICTOR FRANKENSTEIN, looking out a window, with lightning and thunder striking in the distance.

Victor	Who's there? Alas, methought I heard a knock,
	Yet 'twas naught but the rumblings of the storm.
	There, just behind the Jura mountain range,
	Sent from the various quarters of the heav'ns,
	A mighty thunder crashes violently, 5
	Then echoes o'er the miles into my chest.
	Where I should fear, its progress I behold
	With pure delight and curiosity.

[Lightning strikes a tree outside.

	Astounding light! And where the oak tree stood,
	Its mighty limbs unto the sky uprais'd, 10
	Now there is nothing but a blasted stump,
	Mere wooden ribbons flutt'ring in the wind.
	Such wonder—electricity itself—
	Sent by the gods to mortals such as we.

Enter ELIZABETH LAVENZA.

Elizabeth	O Victor, didst thou see the crashing light? 15
Victor	Full well, Elizabeth. The dazzling white
	Was brighter than the stars, the moon, the sun.
Elizabeth	E'en brighter than thy brilliant intellect?
Victor	Yet not as bright as when thou smilest, dear,
	For then is light itself too dark a thing. 20

| Elizabeth | Thou dost but flatter. Ever hast thou done, |
| | Since that first happy day when I arriv'd. |

Victor	No flattery, in sooth, for ev'ry word
	Is but a prologue of what thou deserv'st.
	Ne'er shall the storehouse of my memory 25
	Forget the moment when thou hither cam'st.
	My mother told me, playfully enow,
	That she a pretty present had obtain'd,
	Which should be mine upon the sun's next rise.
	When, on the morrow, she presented thee, 30
	I took her at her word: my promis'd gift,
	So wert thou then and art thou now and wilt
	Thou be tomorrow—to be cherish'd, lov'd,
	Protected by thy Victor evermore.
	The beautiful, ador'd companion of 35
	Mine occupations and my pleasures all—
	So art thou, marvelous Elizabeth,
	Whom I call cousin and shall yet call wife.

Elizabeth	How shall I pass the time when thou art gone
	To Ingolstadt? Who else will speak me such 40
	Sweet words when thou art from Geneva gone?

| Victor | Would I could university avoid. |

Elizabeth	Nay, there thou speakest like a courtier
	Who lies unto the queen for his own gain.
	Thy loyalty to me is only topp'd 45
	By thine unceasing curiosity.
	To learn the hidden laws of nature gives
	Thee gladness that's akin to rapture. This
	Was ever true, e'en since thou wert a lad,
	And ever did I think thee better for 't. 50
	Speak, then, no ill of Ingolstadt, I pray,

| | For thy matriculation is no less
             Than the fulfillment of thine ev'ry hope. | |
|------------|---|---|

Victor   E'er didst thou understand my nature true,
            And know me better than I know myself.   55

Enter HENRY CLERVAL.

Henry   Well met, friends!

Elizabeth   —Henry!

Victor   —Clerval! Welcome, lad.

Henry   I hope I've not disturb'd a tender scene,
            The antidote unto the raging storm.

Elizabeth   Nay, 'tis of thee that we were speaking, Henry.

Henry   Indeed?

Victor   [*aside:*] —Indeed?

Elizabeth   —My Victor was afraid   60
            That, sans his company, my lonely heart
            Would wither whilst he is in Ingoldstadt.
            Would that another friend I could acquire—
            Of fancy and of talent singular,
            Who loveth enterprise and danger both,   65
            Composeth songs heroic, writeth tales
            Of strange enchantments and adventure, too.

Victor   Ah, yea! Perhaps thou knowest, Henry, where
            We'll find a kind companion for my lass—
            A man of chivalry and valiant heart,   70

	Whose wont is to engage his patient friends	
	In playing masquerades of his devising,	
	Who passes time in dressing up his mates	
	As Arthur's knights of the Round Table bold.	
	Would that such an attendant could be found	75
	For my Elizabeth when I depart!	
Henry	Mock me ye may, yet never shall my cheeks	
	Feel that embarrass'd heat and know the blush	
	Of people who are by their dreams asham'd.	
	The busy stage of life, the virtues of	80
	The greatest heroes are my daily theme.	
	And if—by being sweet Elizabeth's	
	Companion, whilst thou off to study runn'st—	
	I shall one day have my name written as	
	A gallant benefactor of our species,	85
	I'll gladly undertake the pleasant task.	
Elizabeth	Ha! Well responded, Henry.	
Victor	—By my troth,	
	In friendship am I wealthy sans compeer.	
Henry	Be careful, ere thou shalt begin to weep	
	And drown us in a sea of salty tears.	90
	Have cheer, my friend. Thou art the best of us,	
	And wilt thy rightful prominence assume	
	When thou in Ingolstadt dost make thy name.	
Elizabeth	Too true! My brilliant cousin and my heart.	
Victor	My preparations I must make anon;	95
	The day of my departure draweth nigh.	
Henry	We'll leave thee to it.	

Elizabeth	—Henry, shall we walk?	

[Exeunt Elizabeth and Henry.

Victor	Perdition catch my soul, but I love them, And would be lost without the jolly pair.	

He begins packing books into a satchel and opens one to read it. Enter ALPHONSE FRANKENSTEIN.

Alphonse	Good day, son.	
Victor	—Holla, father.	
Alphonse	—I observe By this, thy satchel, that thou dost prepare To journey unto Ingolstadt anon. Yet, by the book thou holdst afore thine eyes, I see that—like myself—thou canst not help But scan a fav'rite passage.	100
Victor	—Truly, sir, The books do beckon with a siren's call.	105
Alphonse	And happy is the mariner who heeds. What volume dost thou read?	
Victor	—A slender tome Of natural philosophy, by one Cornelius Agrippa. At first glance, I studied it with weary apathy. The theory that he demonstrateth, though, And facts most wonderful that he relates Hath turn'd my feeling to enthusiasm.	110

Alphonse	Cornelius Agrippa? Victor, dear,	115
	Waste not thy time upon this—'tis sad trash.	
	Thine intellect needs better meat to feed	
	Upon than this. Ah, with the talk of meat,	
	Mine errand unto thee have I recall'd:	
	Come thou at once to supper, all's prepar'd.	120

[Exit Alphonse.

Victor	My father's too-harsh words about the book	
	Run contrary unto his purpose here.	
	The passion for Agrippa he doth seek	
	To dampen hath been fully stok'd instead.	
	With great avidity this book I'll read,	125
	For it may yet inform my future need.	

[Exit.

SCENE 2.
Geneva. The Frankenstein household.

Enter ELIZABETH LAVENZA.

Elizabeth	O, what a noble lady's here o'erthrown!	
	She, my adoptive mother Caroline—	
	Who waited on me hand and foot whilst I	
	Did suffer by the scarlet fever's lash—	
	Hath ta'en the illness from me, e'en as one	5
	Who helps another with a heavy load,	
	Then falls beneath the strain of it at last.	
	Though many arguments were made to her,	
	Entreating her to stay without the room,	
	When she heard that my life was under threat—	10
	I, whom she ever call'd her favorite—	

> She could not, would not, be deterr'd therefrom.
> In nursing me to health again, I fear
> She hath bestow'd a treasure ultimate.

She moves to CAROLINE's chamber. Enter VICTOR, ALPHONSE, and WILLIAM FRANKENSTEIN. Enter CAROLINE BEAUFORT FRANKENSTEIN, abed.

Victor	How is it with thee, mother?	
William	—All are here.	15
Caroline	Elizabeth and Victor, draw ye near:	
	My firmest hopes of future happiness	
	Were plac'd upon the prospect of your union.	
	This expectation to thy father moves,	
	And shall provide his consolation true.	20
	Elizabeth, my love, thou must supply	
	A mother's place unto thy younger kin.	
	'Tis my regret that I am ta'en from you,	
	For, happy and belov'd as I have been,	
	'Tis difficult to take my final leave.	25
	Let these too ill-befitting thoughts depart—	
	Most cheerfully to death I'll lead the way,	
	And hope to meet you in another world.	

[She dies.

Victor	Death cometh for us all, yet how I wish	
	It never would have stopp'd at mother's door.	30
Elizabeth	Beg pardon, Victor, for 'twas my disease	
	Which caught our mother in its deadly net.	
William	Nay, nay, Elizabeth.	

Victor	—Ne'er think it, chuck.	
Alphonse	No reason, argument, or force could keep	
	The lady from her ailing children's side.	35
	Had she the choice again, she'd choose the same.	
	[*To Victor:*] Nor did she wish to keep thee from thy school.	
Victor	Nay, father, surely Ingolstadt shall wait.	
Alphonse	The very thought is disobedient	
	Unto the wishes of thy mother, son.	40
	At week's end, thou to Ingolstadt shall go,	
	Fulfilling ev'ry hope she had for thee.	
Victor	If 'tis her will, thy will, then I shall go.	
Alphonse	Come, William, let us call upon the doctor,	
	And tell him she doth rest at last.	
William	—Yea, sir.	45

[*Exeunt Alphonse and William. Victor and Elizabeth walk out of Caroline's chamber.*]

Elizabeth	'Tis so, then: thy departure follows hard	
	Upon her death. It is decided.	
Victor	—Yea,	
	Though, by my troth, 'tis nearly sacrilege	
	To leave the house, still bath'd in mourning hues,	
	And rush anon toward the thick of life.	50

Elizabeth	Thou must, though, find thy strength. So must we all,
	And keep our promises unto the woman
	Who gave her ev'ry moment to our lives.
Victor	Ne'er wert thou so enchanting as th'art now.
Elizabeth	All shall be well. Serve God, love me, and mend. 55
	We shall press on until thou dost return.
	Write often, Victor—tell me of the thoughts
	That grow within thee whilst thou studiest.
Victor	Each day and more, Elizabeth, I vow.
Elizabeth	Tonight, though, we're together, and may feast 60
	Upon the fruits of friendship, hope, and love.
	Until the time for thy departure comes,
	Let us be merry, sorrow keep at bay.
Victor	Remarkable thou art, best of us all.
	I shall not speak that closing word, "Farewell." 65
	It hath a tone too final, like death's knell.

[Exit Victor.

Elizabeth	Alone again, yet ne'er again alone—
	This family, which rais'd me, brought me in,
	Is now more dear to me than life itself.
	When I from Italy was hither brought, 70
	An orphan taken from her native land,
	Both fear and eagerness were in my heart.
	The years, though, smooth'd the nerves of that young lass,
	And show'd her what a family could be,
	A daughter, cousin, wrapp'd in warm embrace. 75
	Within the midst of that familial love,

A deeper love was blossoming, as well.
My Victor, darling of my future hope,
Hath been my constant joy these many years.
Why, then, is my mind fill'd with prescient fear, 80
As if some dreadful portent it discern'd?
The man is brilliant, plainly, but complex:
Although his mind respected is by all—
An as-yet unsurpassèd intellect—
I know a trouble 'neath the surface lies. 85
His fascination with both life and death,
The mysteries of crossing twixt the two,
Are matters that consume him night and day,
Unfathomable waters he would fathom.
I hope his ship shall not break on these waves, 90
His plans be drown'd beneath the boundless depths.
Ye gods, who watch o'er those who sail the sea,
And watch, too, o'er those whom fate beckoneth,
Be with my Victor as he ventures forth.
To Ingolstadt he flies with purpose plain, 95
But to what outcome—sacred or profane?

[Exit.

SCENE 3.
Ingolstadt.

Enter VICTOR FRANKENSTEIN.

Victor   In Ingolstadt at last, and may my course
Directed be by what I find herein.

Enter PROFESSOR KREMPE.

Good day, sir. May I trouble you, I beg?
Know you Professor Krempe, the specialist

	In natural philosophy, who doth	5
	His lessons teach within this hallow'd place?	
	I bid you, where may I his office find?	

Krempe   I know his office and his person both:
            The one is in this hall near which thou walk'st,
            The other standeth 'fore thee even now.   10

Victor   Professor! Mine I apologies I proffer.
            My name, good sir, is Victor Frankenstein.

                                   [They shake hands.

Krempe   Ah, Frankenstein! Thou dost arrive withal
            Both reputation and expectancy.
            'Tis said thou art a reader.

Victor   —Constantly.   15

Krempe   And com'st to study science.

Victor   —Eagerly.

Krempe   Well, at it, then: I prithee tell me, lad,
            Which natural philosophers thou readst?
            The farmer of the mind, ere he would plant
            New seeds that shall enrich the intellect,   20
            Would know the composition of the soil—
            What worms and weeds and seeds reside therein.

Victor   The alchemists have been the latest growth
            Within the fertile humus of my brain.
            Cornelius Agrippa, recently,   25
            Hath set his hoe upon my willing fields.

Krempe	Is't so?
Victor	—'Tis, yea.
Krempe	—Hast thou spent all thy time In studying such nonsense, verily?
Victor	[*aside:*] Alas, this cold reception is not how I did imagine my first moments here. 30 [*To Krempe:*] I have, indeed, sir.
Krempe	—Most unfortunate! Each minute thou hast wasted on those books Is utterly and wholly lost, my boy. Thou hast o'erburden'd thy poor memory With base, exploded systems, useless names. 35 What desert landscape hast thou dwelt within Where none were kind enow t'inform thee that These fancies thou so greedily imbib'st Are full of ancient notions, nothing more? Thou must restart thy scholarship anon, 40 Ere one more step in this direction take. Pray, come thou on the morrow, and I'll give Thee lists of books that shall improve thy mind, And cure thy course of previous missteps.
Victor	It shall be as you say, Professor, yea. 45
Krempe	Make speed unto Professor Waldman next. I left him in his office presently. Whilst I create a syllabus for thee In natural philosophy, he shall Give chemistry instruction unto thee. 50

Victor	My thanks, Professor Krempe. I'll to him now.
Krempe	And Frankenstein, take heed: no more Agrippa!
Victor	Yea, I am chang'd: I'll go sell all those books.

[Exit Krempe.

                  Nay, never shall I so. But with these words,
                  Thus do I ever make such doubters glad.   55
                  For I mine own gain'd knowledge should profane,
                  If I would forfeit what I've read before,
                  Which brings me sport and profit. Now, to Waldman.

He walks inside the hall. Enter PROFESSOR WALDMAN, in his office, speaking with a STUDENT. VICTOR stands aside, listening.

Waldman	[*to student:*] The ancient teachers of this science strange

                  Did promise great impossibilities   60
                  Whilst they perform'd but naught—a lack profound.
                  The modern masters promise very little:
                  They know that metals cannot alter'd be,
                  And life's elixir is a fantasy.
                  Yet these philosophers, whose hands do seem   65
                  Made only for their dabbling in the dirt,
                  Their eyes for poring over crucibles,
                  Have, ne'ertheless, performèd miracles.
                  They penetrate to nature's recesses,
                  Discovering her hiding-places all.   70
                  Unto the very heavens they ascend,
                  In learning how the blood doth circulate
                  And mingle with the air we daily breathe.
                  They almost have acquir'd pow'rs limitless,
                  Commanding, like a Jove, the thunderbolts,   75
                  Or mimicking the earthquake terrible,
                  Or mocking the vast world invisible
                  With its own shadows. Such are scientists.

Victor	[*aside:*] These words—they are the very words of fate!	
Waldman	[*to Victor:*] Come sirrah, darken not my doorframe more.	80
	Who art thou, whose ears gladly overhear Our conversation?	
Victor	—Victor Frankenstein.	
Waldman	A-ha, the long-awaited Frankstein! [*To student:*] Depart, Hicks. Further shall we speak of this.	

[Exit student.

Victor	Your words, sir, sing sweet music to my soul.	85
	Chord after chord doth sound within my mind, Which fills me with one thought, conception, purpose: I shall become your worthy pioneer, Exploring unknown powers, and unfold Unto the world the deepest mysteries	90
	Of all creation. Yea, by heav'n or hell.	
Waldman	Ha! Thine enthusiasm's evident, And if thy reputation tells no lies, Thou wilt an asset be to Ingolstadt. Hast thou already met Professor Krempe?	95
Victor	Indeed, he sent me hither, you to see.	
Waldman	And what impression made he on thee?	
Victor	—Sir, If I may speak my feeling honestly,	

	Our conversation did but disappoint.	
	He ask'd me which philsophers, of late,	100
	My studies have engag'd. Mine answer was	
	The alchemists—Agrippa, recently—	
	Which he met with a visceral contempt.	
Waldman	To those men's indefatigable zeal	
	Today's philosophers indebted are.	105
	They left to us the simpler task, methinks:	
	T'arrange and give new names unto the facts	
	That they in great degree did bring to light.	
	The labors of all people touch'd by genius,	
	E'en if directed most erroneously,	110
	Ne'er fail in ultimately turning to	
	The firm advantage of humanity.	
Victor	Yea, I could not more heartily agree.	
	If you, sir, will but fashion me a list	
	Of modern chemists, I shall study each	115
	Most earnestly and plumb their mysteries.	
	In faith, I felt an unfair prejudice	
	Toward these moderns, yet your learnèd words	
	Have swiftly cur'd me of my fallacy.	
Waldman	To gain a new disciple makes me glad,	120
	And if thine application equals thine	
	Ability, I have no doubt of thy	
	Success. All science furthers our designs:	
	Whilst chemistry is my peculiar study,	
	'Twould foolish be should I neglect the fruit	125
	That grows on other branches known to science.	
	It is a sorry chemist who attends	
	But to that single realm of human thought.	
	If thou wouldst be a man of science, not	
	A mere experimentalist, thou wilt	130

| | Apply with rigor unto ev'ry field
| | Of natural philosophy.

Victor   —I shall,
              For with your help and careful guidance, sir,
              I hear the call of future destiny.
              My thanks, Professor.

Waldman   —Friend as well, I hope.   135

                                                                    [*Exeunt.*

Enter ROBERT WALTON as Chorus.

Robert   At university did Victor thrive,
              And thus the story forward turns two years.
              With progress rapid, he who was a boy
              Is now a man respected and well-train'd.
              So ardently and eagerly he studied   140
              That often stars had disappear'd by light
              Of morning whilst he was engagèd in
              The vital work of his laboratory.

                                                                      [*Exit.*

Enter VICTOR FRANKENSTEIN in his laboratory.

Victor   Whence doth the principle of life proceed?
              That is the question bold, which ever hath   145
              Been left unto the realm of mystery.
              And wherefore is it so? Because around
              The boundaries of life stands life's dark twin.
              If 'tis our aim to know the cause of life,
              We must first have some recourse unto death.   150
              Uncovering these matters is a need

That burns inside my heart an 'twere a fire,
A wildfire shut up in my very bones.
I weary when I try to hold it in—
Forsooth, it proveth most impossible.   155
Anatomy must be my next pursuit,
Therein t'observe the natural decay
Of human flesh, how it corrupted grows,
How—like a peach left too long in the sun—
It shrivels, breaks, returns again to dust.   160
Unto the vaults and charnel-houses shall
I venture sans the slightest twinge of fear.
My father took precautions, that my mind
Should ne'er dread horror supernatural.
Zounds! Should I master sciences as these,   165
The force of nature shall be in my hands!
Soon could I be bestowing animation
On lifeless matter. Yea, with time enow,
I may reverse corruption of a corpse,
Renewing life where death once proudly stood.   170
Bones must I have! Toes! Fingertips as well!
The eyeballs ta'en from our dissecting room
Will fain, I'll warrant, watch my progress with
No little measure of amazement—ha!
How shall my family and comrades in   175
Geneva marvel when they hear of this.
Until then, though, my work must never cease,
E'en if my candle burneth at both ends.
Each night by fever am I sore oppress'd,
And nervous have become to some degree—   180
The fall of leaves begin to startle me,
As if I had been guilty of a crime.
When I do spy me in the looking-glass,
I am alarm'd at what I have become,
Ill-dress'd, unshaven, wretchèd to behold.   185
O, let me not be mad, not mad, sweet heav'n

Keep me in temper: I would not be mad!
Be still; my noble aim sustaineth me.
My labors soon shall end, and thereupon
With exercise and some amusement will 190
I drive away incipient disease.
Invigorating pleasures shall I greet
When my creation is, at last, complete.

[Exit.

SCENE 1.
Ingolstadt.

Enter PROFESSOR KREMPE and PROFESSOR WALDMAN.

Krempe	Ho, Waldman. Hast of late seen Frankenstein?	
	The lad is more dishevel'd than a pig	
	That dineth ev'ry hour amidst the slop.	
	The dark November sky is nothing next	
	To his demeanor, gloomier by half.	5
Waldman	His studies, truly, take him past the point	
	To which the lesser scholars venture. 'Tis	
	A passion that doth move him.	
Krempe	—'Tis obsession!	
	His most unnatural experiments	
	Will sway our younger students.	
Waldman	—Unto what?	10
	Perchance he sways them unto greater truths.	
	And if our students are led by the nose—	
	As asses are—is not the fault our own?	
Krempe	Thou, then, observest naught amiss with him?	
	Young Victor's frequent graveyard visits, with	15
	His horrid mien and shameful stench to match—	
	These trouble thee not in the slightest part?	
Waldman	I merely think we must be circumspect.	
	Give him a chance to prove himself before	
	We deem him utterly unsuitable.	20
Krempe	I like it not, yet will my doubts allay	
	Until we see his thoughts to action lead.	

[Exeunt.

Enter VICTOR FRANKENSTEIN on balcony with the body of THE MONSTER on a table.

Victor	It must be now—proportional the limbs,	
	The features I've selected beautiful.	
	Say not so, though. There's none of beauty here.	25
	All yellow is its skin, scarce covering	
	Large muscles and foul arteries beneath.	
	Its hair a lustrous black, sharp teeth of white,	
	Vile, wat'ry eyes, and lips as dark as night.	
	Eight feet in length—colossal, evil beast.	30

[The monster opens its eyes.

          It's naught but pure catastrophe, forsooth—
          The beauty of the dream I once enjoy'd
          Soon vanisheth, and breathless horror comes.
          A mummy given animation would
          Look not so hideous as this base wretch.   35
          Intensely do its yellow eyes probe me—
          View thy creator, monster, and despair.
          Enow! I'll not endure its aspect longer.

[Exit Frankenstein from the balcony. The monster rises and looks around, grinning, then exits from the balcony.

Enter VICTOR FRANKENSTEIN, below, on the street. Enter HENRY CLERVAL, severally, meeting him.

Henry	Holla, good Victor!	
Victor	—Henry, is it thee?	
	Or do mine eyes some spectral vision see?	40

Henry	How glad I am to see thee, and upon
	The very instant I arriv'd herein.
Victor	Thou art most welcome—in the world entire
	There's none but thee so gladly I'd behold.
Henry	Hast hither come from thy laboratory? 45
	Wouldst thou show me the progress of thy work?
Victor	Nay! [*Aside:*] What if he the monster should observe?
	[*To Henry:*] Nay, nay, although the night is bitter cold,
	With rain that falls from sky most comfortless,
	The air doth suit me well. Pray, let us walk. 50
	Tell me how thou didst leave my family—
	My father, brothers, and Elizabeth.
Henry	They are quite well, though made uneasy that
	They hear of thee so seldom. Verily,
	'Twas mine intention to reprove thee in 55
	This matter. Yet, I now much closer see
	Thy face, thy body—how ill thou appear'st!
	So thin and pale, as though thou hadst the watch
	For sev'ral nights, sans any wink of sleep.
Victor	Thou hast guess'd truly, Henry. Lately hath 60
	One occupation kept me far from rest.
	These harsh employments, though, are at an end.
	Methinks, at length, I am full free. Ha. Ha!
Henry	O Victor, by the wildness in thine eyes
	And heartless, unrestrainèd laughter, I 65
	Am both affrighted and astonishèd.
	Laugh not with such untamèd manner, friend.
	How ill thou art! What is the cause thereof?

Victor	Nay, only he can tell! The monstrous he!	
	Methinks I see Elizabeth just there.	70
	She, in the very bloom of health—look, look!	
	I shall embrace her, kiss her rosy lips.	
	Alack, she turns to grave-worms in mine arms—	
	She is my mother, dead, a rotten corpse!	
	O save me, save me—death doth seize me. Help!	75

[Victor faints.

Henry	My friend, so plagu'd by visions, fits, and fear!
	What signs of hell afore me do appear?

[Exeunt.

SCENE 2.
The woods outside Ingolstadt.

Enter DE LACEY, playing his lute, with AGATHA, FELIX, and SAFIE.

Agatha	Kind father, wilt thou play the song again?	
De Lacey	Of course, my girl. I'd ne'er deny thee song.	
	[*Sings:*] There was a stranger came to town,	
	To-ree, to-ray, to-rah,	
	Yet ev'ry household turn'd him down,	5
	To-ree, to-ray, to-rah.	
	May our hearts ever welcome in,	
	To-ree, to-ray, to-rah,	
	The guest as if 'twere our own kin.	
	To-ree, to-ray, to-rah.	10
Safie	Pray, Felix, wilt thou read again the tome	
	That tells of empires' ruins, with which thou	
	Didst give instruction when I first arriv'd?	

	I'd rather hear the tales of humans past—	
	Their virtue, vices, and magnificence—	15
	Than any book of poetry e'er writ.	

Felix   Indeed, the stories fill my heart as well,
For in their company our love did bloom.

Safie   How fortunate that thou in Paris dwelt
When my ill-fated father came to trial.   20
Thy sense of justice, which I do adore,
Look'd on his execution with contempt,
And could not bear to let him die unjustly.

Felix   I lov'd the man; I love his daughter more.

Agatha   Your story's dearer that the tales within   25
That volume ye oft read together, yea.

Felix   The trials and the tribulations we
Have shar'd would fill a history entire.

De Lacey   [*to Safie:*] How fortunate that thou, my borrow'd daughter,
Did make thy safe return to us in th'end.   30
'Tis ev'rything: we are together, safe.

Agatha   The day is pleasant, though the weather's cool.
Shall we take full advantage of the sun
And walk awhile among the countryside?
The flowers and the fields have rested through   35
The worst of winter—now the daffodils
Are prim'd to burst forth from their earthen graves;
The resurrection of the spring begins.

Felix   Thou wilt turn poet, Agatha. [*To Safie:*] Wouldst walk?

Safie	Yea, naturally, with thee by my side.	40

Agatha	Sweet father, thou wilt join?

De Lacey   —Nay, children mine.
Th'exertion of the morning makes me tir'd.
I'd gladly rest awhile.

Agatha   —'Tis well. We'll find
Thee flow'rs, and we'll deliver thee the scent
Of early springtime's bounty presently.   45

[She kisses De Lacey on the head. Exeunt Agatha, Felix, and Safie.

Enter THE MONSTER aside, hidden.

Monster   Words, words, words! With these rough-hewn, ink-
                                                          black lips
And this brain rumbling in my wrinkl'd pate,
This family have I observ'd for weeks,
And from them learn'd the gift of human speech.
My memories of my creation are   50
Like shadows dim, confus'd and indistinct.
Such strange sensations seiz'd upon me, then—
I saw, felt, heard, and smelt concurrently—
A burst of senses such that it was long
Before I could distinguish one from th'other.   55
A darkness was upon me, calm and still,
Until, by opening mine eyes, the light
Oppressively did pour in on my sight.
My maker having fled the premises,
I rais'd my body, drawing to its height,   60
And—like an infant braving its new world—
Took my first steps, uncertain and alone.
I pass'd the boundaries of Ingolstadt,

And haply wander'd to the forest here.
One day, too near a cottage did I roam, 65
Whereon some people spied my horrid mien—
The children shriek'd. A woman, fainting, dropp'd.
The village whole was rous'd—some folk took flight,
Whilst some attack'd me. Injur'd grievously
By stones and other weapons ta'en to hand, 70
I thither fled into the open country,
And cower'd fearfully in hovel low.
This hovel, which hath been my home since then,
Is near the cottage where this fam'ly dwells.
Soon I beheld the girl, her father blind— 75
Who on his lute habitually play'd—
Her brother, and his lovely paramour.
How I have long'd to join them, but dar'd not.
The family in poverty do dwell,
Yet in each other find abundant joy. 80
My custom it became to bring them wood,
Delivering large stacks whilst they did sleep,
Delighting in the cheer it brought to them.
I form'd in mine imagination keen
Some thousand pictures of the moment when 85
I would present myself to them at last,
And how they would receive mine overtures.
Initially, they would disgusted be,
Until, by kind demeanor and a speech
Of words conciliating should I win 90
Their favor first, and afterward their love.
The moment for this undertaking comes—
The old man is alone. My voice, though harsh,
Hath nothing terrible within its sound.
In th'absence of his children I may gain 95
The swift good will and mediation of
De Lacey, by which means I may secure
The toleration of the younger set.

[De Lacey plays his guitar again.

De Lacey	[*sings:*] When I was young,	
	And life was new,	100
	Then had I joy,	
	Then had I you.	
	When I was young,	
	Knew not the cost,	
	I was unkind	105
	And you were lost.	
	Now am I old,	
	And you, my pet,	
	Are, verily,	
	My sole regret.	110

[The monster knocks on De Lacey's cottage door.

                      Who calleth, rapping at my chamber door?

Monster	Beg pardon for th'intrusion, worthy sir.	
	I am a traveler in want of rest.	
	'Twould be most kind if I may, by your fire,	
	Take rest some minutes ere I journey on.	115
De Lacey	Come in, and if I may relieve your wants	
	'Twill be my pleasure. Yet, my children are	
	Away, and I am blind. I therefore shall	
	Have difficulty proffering a meal.	

[The monster enters and sits.

Monster	You are too kind—enow of food have I.	120
	Of warmth and respite am I most in need.	

[DeLacey sits across from the monster.

De Lacey	Your language, stranger, is the selfsame tongue	
	My family and I most often speak—	
	Are you of France?	

Monster	—Your ears do you much credit.	
	Yet nay, no Frenchman I, though I receiv'd	125
	Mine education from a family	
	That came from France. My journey's endpoint is	
	The warm protection of a group of folk,	
	Whom I sincerely love, forsooth, and on	
	Whose favor all my future hopes depend.	130
	Perchance my tale shall move your spirit, sir:	
	I am a creature most unfortunate,	
	Deserted, sans a friend upon the earth,	
	Relations none that I may call upon.	
	The people unto whom I venture now	135
	Have ne'er laid eyes on me and know me not.	
	In troth, my heart's a ship upon the waves,	
	Which fears a present wreck on shallow rocks.	
	For, if I fail with them, I'll live fore'er	
	Like Cain—an outcast in the world's regard.	140

De Lacey	Do not despair. 'Tis most lamentable	
	To find oneself both friendless and alone,	
	Yet I believe the hearts of people—when	
	Unprejudic'd by mere self-interest—	
	Are full of love toward each other and	145
	Inclin'd to charity. Upon your hopes	
	And on these unknown friends of yours rely.	

Monster	They are most kind, of upright character,	
	Yet hold some prejudice against me still.	
	My disposition is toward the good,	150
	My life hath hitherto been innocent,	
	Yea free from harm and beneficial, too.

	A preconception doth remain, I fear,	
	Which clouds their eyes. The tragic consequence	
	Is that where they should see a friend in need,	155
	Naught but a monster shall their eyes behold.	
De Lacey	Most tragic, yea. But if you blameless are,	
	Is there not something you can say to them	
	To undeceive their sympathetic hearts?	
Monster	It is that hope that spurs my present quest,	160
	Which gives me hope and fear in equal parts.	
	I love these friends and, unbeknownst to them,	
	Have many months done daily kindnesses	
	Toward them.	
De Lacey	—Whereabouts do they reside?	
Monster	Quite near the very spot whereon we speak.	165
De Lacey	If you will unto me your tale confide,	
	I may assist in helping them see reason.	
	Though I am blind and cannot see your face,	
	Your words persuade me that you are sincere.	
	'Twould bring me joy to be of service thus.	170
Monster	Your offer I most gratefully receive!	
	My thanks for your assistance and belief.	
	By kindness you shall raise me from the dust.	
	Your benefaction doth assure me of	
	Success with those whom I shall meet anon.	175
De Lacey	What are their names and addresses, I pray?	
Monster	[*aside:*] This is the moment—if I speak the truth—	
	That either shall ensure my future days	

                    Or horribly undo me. [*To De Lacey:*] Sir, protect me!
                    'Tis you and your good family I seek.   180
                    Do not desert me in my hour of need!

          [The monster kneels before De Lacey, holding his hands.

De Lacey   By heaven! Tell me who you are at once!

     Enter AGATHA, FELIX, and SAFIE, returning from their walk.

Felix   Angels and ministers of grace defend us!

Safie   A monster! What a horrid, ugly rogue!

Agatha   He doth attack our father. Felix, help!   185

*[Felix rushes to the monster and tears him away from De Lacey, then hits the
                              monster with a walking stick.*

Monster   Mine only friends! O, be ye not so harsh!

Agatha   No friends of yours, who would our father slay.
            Vile wretch!

Safie   —Intruder!

Felix   —Crude, insensate beast!

Monster   I only e'er desir'd your kind regard!
            Not this reception, made of pain and hate.   190
            You taught me language; and my profit on't
            Is, I know how to curse. Your actions shall
            Return to haunt you—I shall be your bane!

                              [Exit monster, running away.

Agatha	Speak, father art thou well?
De Lacey	—Yea, Agatha. What was it, children? What did ye behold? 195
Safie	A hellish monster none could e'er describe, As only darkest nightmares could conceive.
Agatha	Art certain that the brute abus'd thee not?
De Lacey	Nay, not at all. In faith, he did appear In guise of friendship. 'Tis astonishing 200 To hear your words, describing he whom I Assum'd was but a pilgrim seeking help.
Safie	The devil may the form of th'angels take.
De Lacey	Methought him neither angel nor a devil, But sad and reaching out in friendship's name. 205
Felix	'Tis certain, father, thou art much disturb'd— This was no friend, but fiend who haunted thee. This cottage we cannot inhabit more, For thy life—all our lives—are in grave peril. This horror shall be with us evermore, 210 And we must fly to save our very souls.
Agatha	Farewell then, house—another home we'll find.

[Exeunt Agatha, De Lacey, Felix, and Safie.

Enter THE MONSTER, holding a lit torch.

Monster	Why did I live? Curs'd in creation I!
So wantonly was life bestow'd on me—
I should have taken arms against a sea   215
Of troubles and destroy'd my very self.
But, failing that, I shall have my revenge.
Rage doth o'ercome my heart, if any heart
Doth beat within my wither'd, borrow'd breast.
These friends of mine—not friends, no, not that
                                                        word,   220
But hateful, prejudicial enemies—
Hath fled and gone or they would be swept up
Within my all-consuming, righteous ire.
I'll burn their house, wherein I mercy sought,
Until there's naught but cinders that remain.   225
Come wind, and fan the flames of mine intent,
And fire come purge the painful memory.
                    [He lights the cottage on fire.
Now where? My next step shall decide my fate.
I have it: I shall my creator find
And set his world aglow as he did mine—   230
The justice of it pleases very well.
Toward my maker shall I bend my path,
Engulfing him within my fiery wrath.

                                                   [Exit.

SCENE 3.
Ingolstadt.

*Enter VICTOR FRANKENSTEIN, in bed, and HENRY CLERVAL
waiting on him.*

Victor	My senses only now return'd to me—
Yet how long, Henry, did I lie abed?

Henry	'Tis many months, my friend, thou hast been ill.	
	It does me well to see thee so restor'd.	
	Thy body was by much exhaustion rent,	5
	And from thy lips mere ravings issu'd forth.	
	Thine illness and thy frame of mind put thoughts	
	Of taking thee unto Geneva out—	
	The journey homeward was impossible.	
	'Twas also better to keep full report	10
	Of thy grave illness from thy father and	
	Elizabeth, who would but worry so.	
	Thy father being most unfit to travel,	
	'Twas necessary that I should conceal	
	The true degree of thy disorder. Thus,	15
	In kindness unto them and thee alike,	
	They know naught of thy sickness' extent,	
	But only that thou hast been ill.	
Victor	—Wise friend,	
	But little have I all thy care deserv'd.	
	How kind, how very good thou art to me.	20
	This winter, whilst in study thou shouldst labor—	
	Which, verily, thou promis'dst to thyself—	
	Thou wert within my sick room long consum'd.	
	How shall I make my recompense to thee?	
Henry	Thy payment shall be paid in full an thou	25
	Wilt no more decompose thyself, but thrive—	
	Regain thy health as fast as possible.	
	Whilst thou art in high spirits, Victor, may	
	I speak upon one subject with thee, friend?	
Victor	[*aside:*] Alas, what awful subject can he mean?	30
	Doth he allude to that most horrible	
	Of themes, on which I dare not even think?

Henry	Thou, Victor, turnest such a shade of green	
	That I do fear thou plungest to the depths.	
	Compose thyself—I shall not mention it	35
	If 'tis so agitating to thy mind.	
	'Twas only this: thy cousin and thy father	
	Would be most comforted should they receive	
	A letter writ by thine own hand. As they	
	Are ignorant of all thou underwent'st,	40
	They grow uneasy at thy silence long.	
Victor	Naught but this matter, Henry, verily?	
	Pray, be assur'd: my first and foremost thoughts	
	Fly unto those who are most dear to me.	
Henry	Thou shalt then, welcome what I have for thee:	45
	A letter from thy priz'd Elizabeth.	

[Henry hands Victor a letter, which Victor reads.

Enter ELIZABETH on balcony.

Elizabeth	My dearest cousin, thou hast long been ill,	
	And even Henry's frequent letters prove	
	Inadequate, my mind to reassure.	
	Of late, he doth report thou growest stronger—	50
	My fondest hope is to receive such news	
	From thine own hand. Get well, and make return.	
	Here shalt thou find a cheerful home and friends	
	Who love thee dearly. We are keeping well:	
	Young Ernest, now sixteen, is full of vim,	55
	And plans to join the foreign service soon.	
	Dost thou recall Justine, the girl who came	
	To live with us when she was twelve years old?	
	Her father having died most tragic'lly,	

> Justine's foul mother view'd her with contempt. 60
> Both were most pleas'd to have her live with us—
> A happy and frank-hearted girl is she,
> Addition welcome to our growing home.
> She was much griev'd by thy kind mother's death,
> Yet more of death Justine would know anon. 65
> Some months from thy departure, she was call'd
> Once more unto her ill, repentant mother.
> Justine did weep to leave our pleasant house,
> And found but little joy when she return'd
> Unto her mother, who, at times, did beg 70
> Justine's forgiveness for her former self,
> But—like a feather blowing in the wind,
> Which changeth course upon the slightest breeze—
> Her mother's mood oft turn'd once more to rage,
> Accusing our Justine of horrid crimes. 75
> The end is this, for too long runs my tale:
> Of late, her mother died, and Justine is
> Return'd again, to general relief.
> Last shall I write of William—darling boy—
> He, youngest of thy brothers, keepeth well, 80
> His laughing eyes of blue, eyelashes dark,
> Sweet dimples which appear upon his cheeks,
> And curly hair proclaim a ruddy boy.
> In short, sweet Victor, all Geneva thrives,
> Except that thou art ill and we do long 85
> To hear, in thine own words, that thou improv'st.
> One line—one word—shall be a blessing, love.
> I am thy cousin and thy paramour,
> Who waits for three with expectation great.
>
> *[Exit Elizabeth.*

Victor   Elizabeth, my dear and noble lass!   90
              Pass me a quill, good Henry sans delay—

| | I'll write them presently that I might ease | |
| | Their too-prolong'd concern for me. | |

Henry   —Hurrah!

[Henry hands Victor a quill and paper, and Victor begins writing.

Enter PROFESSOR KREMPE and PROFESSOR WALDMAN.

Krempe   Young Clerval, speak: how doth the patient fare?

Henry   Professors, you are welcome. Witness, sirs: 95
          Strong Victor writeth to his family,
          Informing them of his recovery.

Waldman   'Tis well! Ho, Frankenstein, we were dismay'd:
          Thou hast made progress most astonishing
          In all the sciences. To lose thy skill   100
          Would be a loss to th'university.

Victor   The sciences? Endeavor horrible.

Waldman   What means this utterance?

Krempe   —He is unwell,
          And likely knows not yet whereon he speaks.
          Admitting this doth give me little joy,   105
          But thou hast, naughty lad, outstripp'd us all.
          A youngster who, but some few years ago,
          Did hold Agrippa as the gospel truth,
          Has set himself above the body of
          The university, and now is head!   110

Victor   O, say not so.

Krempe	—Thy modesty is plain,
	A quality most excellent in youth.
	Yet quickly doth its charm begin to wane.
	Thou art a master, Frankenstein, and should—
	As soon as thou art capable enow— 115
	Claim ev'ry honor for which thou wert born.
Victor	No more of this, no more!

[*Waldman and Krempe look on in shock.*

Henry	—Professors, please:
	My friend is only just this morning come
	To consciousness, and still may ailing be.
	Too much of sudden pressure is not well 120
	For one whose mind and body have been tax'd
	As his most surely have these many months.
Waldman	We shall remove ourselves at once. Come, Krempe—
	Let us get hence that he may swiftly heal.
	[*To Victor:*] Thy prospects are abundant, lad, in
	sooth, 125
	All science looks to thee for wonders vast.

[*Exeunt Krempe and Waldman.*

Victor	Lock thou the door, I bid thee, Henry.
Henry	—Why?
	What specter haunteth thee that, at their words—
	Which are so full of compliment and praise
	That any student would be glad to hear— 130
	Thou dost but shrink as one who was accus'd
	Or threaten'd with a punishment severe?

Victor	Great pow'r brings great responsibility,	
	Which once I did desire, but now no more.	
	If, Henry, thou shalt prove a friend to me,	135
	Help me regain my strength that I, with haste,	
	May journey to Geneva, to my home.	
Henry	Mine efforts I've expended for thy health,	
	And shall not stop them now thou growest stronger.	
	Instead, together shall we toil that thou	140
	Mayst—like proud Samson, when his hair regrew—	
	Renew the strength that heav'n hath given thee.	
Victor	Thou callest forth the better feelings of	
	My heart and teachest my soul how to cheer.	
Henry	Sincerely do I love thee, Victor, and	145
	Shall elevate thy ailing mind until	
	It doth surpass the might it had before.	
	Mine earnest hope is but to see thee whole.	
Victor	With this, my former sins are near forgot—	
	My thanks for ev'ry good that thou hast wrought.	150

[Exeunt.

SCENE 4.

The outskirts of Geneva. A forest, near a river.

Enter THE MONSTER.

Monster	Now am I in Geneva, here to bring
	Disaster on he who created me,
	Unmaking my foul maker with delight.
	The mildness of my nature left behind,

| | I am turn'd gall and bitterness entire. 5
| | Though I know not where he who made me dwells,
| | With some sixth sense my spirit pushes forward.
| | Hark! Footsteps make approach—thus must I hide
| | Or else my purpose too soon is reveal'd.

He hides. Enter JUSTINE MORITZ, running and laughing.

Justine   [*aside:*] Ha, William—never shalt thou catch me here! 10
           My legs are long and swift as a gazelle,
           Which o'er the fields and plains doth bound with ease.
           The lad is in my care the day entire,
           So must I seek out quiet moments when
           He is not, shadow-like, e'er by my side. 15
                              [*She approaches the river.*
           The water is too deep and fast to cross,
           Yet near the bank I shall conceal myself
           To frighten William when he hither comes.
           Climb down, reach out my foot and—O, alack!

[Justine slips and falls into the river. The monster comes out of hiding.

Monster   Frivolity turn'd folly in a trice! 20
           The lass is drawn beneath the waters' foam,
           And none shall serve as rescuer but I.

[He moves quickly and pulls Justine, unconscious, from the water.

Enter WILLIAM FRANKENSTEIN, not seeing them yet.

William   Justine, where art thou gone? I'll find thee yet!

Monster   [*aside:*] 'Tis well. This lovely child—who must be he
           From whom this youthful woman hid herself— 25

　　　　　　　　Hath surely liv'd too briefly on the earth
　　　　　　　　To form the prejudices of his elders
　　　　　　　　Or know a horror of deformity.
　　　　　　　　Belike to mine entreaty he'll give ear,
　　　　　　　　And I shall educate him as my friend,　　　　30
　　　　　　　　Thus not to be alone and desolate.

　　　　　　　　　　　　　　　　　[*The monster steps forward.*

William　　　　Help, ho! A ghoul, a goblin! Help, alack!

　　　　　　　　　　[*The monster places his hands on the boy gently.*

Monster　　　　What mean'st thou by this, boy? I mean no harm.
　　　　　　　　I prithee, hear my words.

William　　　　　　—Unhand me, beast!
　　　　　　　　Thou monster, ugly wretch, and ogre vile!　　　35
　　　　　　　　Sans doubt, thou wish'st to eat me and take joy
　　　　　　　　In tearing my young body limb from limb!
　　　　　　　　Release me, or my father I shall tell!

Monster　　　　Perforce thou wilt not see thy father soon,
　　　　　　　　But come withal that I may teach thee much.　　40

William　　　　Let go, thou hideous, repulsive swine!
　　　　　　　　I am the son of Alphonse Frankenstein,
　　　　　　　　A syndic of these parts, respected much,
　　　　　　　　Who shall see fit to punish thee anon.
　　　　　　　　Thou dar'st not keep me; it may cost thy life!　　45

Monster　　　　Thou art a Frankenstein, in sooth? A lad
　　　　　　　　By any other name would smell more sweet,
　　　　　　　　But thy name—Frankenstein—becomes thy curse.
　　　　　　　　Thou dost belong unto mine enemy,

	And shalt become the first to feel my wrath,	50
	The op'ning act that sets the stage for death,	
	Initial victim of my righteous fire!	

William   Nay, devil! Shag-hair'd villain! Fie upon
Thee!

[The monster moves his hands to William's neck and starts strangling him.

Monster   —What, thou egg! Young fry of treachery!
Is this th'reward for my benevolence?   55
I sav'd a human being from destruction,
And for my recompense I writhe beneath
The verbal bullets of a schoolboy's pistol?
Whatever recent mood of gentleness,
Or milk of human kindness—which was mine   60
Mere moments hence—hath fled and gone fore'er.
Come hellish rage, come gnashing of my teeth—
Eternal hatred and horrific vengeance
Unto all humankind I hereby vow!

[William dies, and the monster drops his body to the ground. The monster takes a locket from around William's neck and places it in Justine's pocket. Exit monster. Justine awakes.

Justine   The forest and the river and its bank—   65
These pastoral surroundings I recall,
Yet little else of why I here awake.
My memory is like a foggy morn,
When e'en the whitest sheep within the glade
Cannot be seen till nearly tripp'd upon.   70
Some glimpses, though, are breaking through the mist:
Young William was my charge, and we did run
Toward the river, where... There mem'ry fails.
Yet where is William? Surely is he near.

> *[Justine looks around and spots William.*

Ho, lad! Methought we separated were, 75
Yet now I've found thee, or thou foundest me.
But wherefore wilt thou not give voice to me—
Art thou asleep? Have we been here so long?

> *[She gets closer to him and sees his face.*

By heaven, what a misery here lies!
My boy, my lad, the pride of Frankenstein— 80
Thine eyes ope wide, thy mouth stretch'd horribly,
As if thou wouldst call out in justice's name,
And shriek to tell the world how thou wert slain.
O, mask of death, both twisted and perverse!
How shall I this foul scene of death explain, 85
Since I know naught of what hath here befall'n?
Is't possible I am to blame for this?
The child was my responsibility.
Today was I his only nurturer,
Who should against his murd'rer shut the door, 90
Not put my hands around his neck myself.
Am I turn'd accidental murderer?
Would that I could remember what hath pass'd.
Methinks I somehow have this lad betray'd.
O cursèd fate, which knocketh at my door, 95
And bears transgressions I must answer for!

> *[Exit.*

SCENE 1.

Geneva. The Frankenstein household.

Enter ERNEST FRANKENSTEIN and ELIZABETH LAVENZA.

Elizabeth	Long have we search'd—alas, to profit none.
	Where could our William and Justine have gone?
Ernest	I heard them playing joyf'lly yesterday,
	Midst hiding games they wander'd from the house.
	When they did not appear at suppertime, 5
	Methought for certain they would soon return.
Elizabeth	So did I, too, yet now the night hath pass'd.
	And something in my heart discomfits me.
Ernest	Fear not, Elizabeth. All shall be well.

Enter ALPHONSE FRANKENSTEIN, carrying WILLIAM's body.

Alphonse	Woe, woe! Our little boy is ta'en away. 10
Elizabeth	Hast found him, father? Is the poor lad ill?
Alphonse	Still damp, expos'd to all the dews of night,
	The boy's at rest fore'er.
Ernest	—Not dead?
Alphonse	—E'en so.

[Alphonse sets William's body down, and Elizabeth rushes to inspect it.

Elizabeth	Alas, our darling child I've murderèd!
	See—marks upon his alabaster neck, 15

	The purplish prints of fingers thereupon.
	His flame extinguish'd most unnat'rally!

[She faints. Ernest runs to her side.

Alphonse	Elizabeth!

Ernest	—Dear cousin, rouse thyself!
	Too much of misery have we today.
	Thy loss would prove too much for us to bear. 20

Alphonse	To Victor I must write without delay,
	That he may join us in our time of woe.

Elizabeth	[*waking:*] Sweet William, all the fault doth lie on me
	For thy most tragic and untimely death.

Ernest	Soft thee! How could it be, Elizabeth? 25

Elizabeth	'Twas not two days ago that William hath
	Begg'd me to wear his mother's miniature,
	Which in a locket I am wont to wear.
	Most valuable it was, and yesternight
	Discover'd I 'twas missing from my room. 30
	Young William must have taken it therefrom
	And tempted someone to this rash misdeed.

Alphonse	Nay, never think it. Be thou comforted.
	Come, Victor must hear swiftly of our plight.

[Exeunt.

Enter VICTOR FRANKENSTEIN on balcony, holding a letter, with
HENRY CLERVAL.

Henry	What is the content thou dost read therein	35
	That turns thy visage such a pallid shade?	

Victor   Read, Henry, if thou hast the strength for it.

[Victor hands Henry the letter, and Henry reads it.

Henry   Not William, he the youngest Frankenstein—
Shall such a hearty branch be cut so soon?
No consolation can I offer thee;   40
This rank disaster is irrep'rable.
What wilt thou do?

Victor   —Get hence unto Geneva.
My spirit knows no end to its despair,
Its mourning for the child who brighter shone
Than any star within the firmament.   45

Henry   Now sleeps he with his angel mother, Victor.
Who that had seen him, in young beauty's joy,
But would not weep o'er his too-early death?
And more than this—to feel the murd'rer's grasp.
O, rogue who could destroy such innocence,   50
Whose radiance we often baskèd in.
'Tis comfort weak to know that, though we mourn,
He is at rest, his pangs are at an end,
His suffering forever banishèd.
The sod shall cover o'er his gentle form,   55
Releasing him from pain. No longer shall
He be a subject for our pity, nay—
That is reserv'd henceforth for those bleak folk
Who mis'rably are his survivors call'd.

Victor	'Tis so. Brave Henry, glad I am that thou	60
	Art with me in this most severe of times.	
Henry	Pray, get thee gone unto Geneva, friend—	
	Be with the family that needs thee now.	

[They embrace. Exit Victor from balcony.

Why should these decent, worthy people face
Such torments? First, the mother too-soon ta'en   65
By such a swift and horrible disease,
And now, kind William, lad of many hopes,
Is touch'd by evil such as I'd not name.
O wretchèd friends, unhappy Frankensteins!
Doom falls not fairly on this family.   70

[Exit Henry from balcony.

Enter VICTOR FRANKENSTEIN below, near his home. A storm can be heard.

Victor Obscurely do I see, as through a glass,
The desolation of my destiny—
It seems some apparition follows me
That would, 'mongst humans, make me basest yet.
Behold this tempest that doth shake the world,   75
So beautiful and terrifying both.
Dear angel William, 'tis thy funeral,
The dirge that nature singeth to thy soul.

Enter THE MONSTER, at a distance.

Monster [*aside:*] My maker hath return'd to home at last.
A gruesome welcome I've prepar'd for him!   80

[Exit monster.

| Victor | Nay, nay, it cannot be! The lightning's flash
| | Illuminates an object palpably:
| | Gigantic stature, aspect most deform'd,
| | More hideous than all humanity—
| | 'Tis that same fiend to whom I granted life! 85
| | O how the truth doth o'er my senses sweep,
| | As if I were the ark and it the flood—
| | He was the most unhuman murderer
| | Of our dear William—yea, 'tis passing plain!
| | The instant that the notion flies to mind, 90
| | It is confirm'd by ev'ry thinking sense.
| | I should pursue the demon presently,
| | Yet he is too far gone to catch him up—
| | Instead, to home I'll go sans further wait.

He enters his house. Enter ERNEST FRANKENSTEIN.

| Ernest | O, dearest Victor, welcome home at last! 95
| | Yet, I could hope 'twas three months earlier—
| | Then hadst thou found us joyous and delighted.
| | Thou comest now to share a misery
| | Which nothing can alleviate, I fear.
| | At least thy presence shall revive our father, 100
| | Who sinks beneath misfortune gloomily,
| | As if he were an anchor, grief the sea.
| | Perchance thy keen persuasion shall induce
| | Elizabeth to cease her tormenting
| | Self-accusations. Much doth rest on thee! 105
| | Apologies—this welcome is abrupt.

| Victor | What is the cause that doth distress her so?

| Ernest | She most some consolation doth require,
| | For she believes she caus'd the horrid death

	Of our dear William. She'll no reason hear,	110
	E'en though the murderer discover'd is—	
Victor	The murderer discover'd? Is it so?	
	By heav'n, how can it be? Who would attempt,	
	The brigand to pursue? Impossible!	
	One may as well pursue the very wind,	115
	Or stop a mountain stream withal a straw.	
	I saw the rogue; he moments hence was free!	
Ernest	Thy answer, sir, is enigmatical.	
	Discovery completeth misery,	
	And none the revelation would believe	120
	When first 'twas verified. For who would think	
	Our good Justine, so fond and amiable,	
	Could on the instant capable become	
	Of such a frightful and appalling crime?	
Victor	Our Justine Moritz? Doth she stand accus'd?	125
	'Tis wrongful, troth. None could suppose it true.	
Ernest	At first, none did, yet circumstances hath	
	Near forc'd conviction on our better sense.	
	Her own behavior, too, is so confus'd	
	That little room remaineth for our doubts.	130
	She shall be tried upon tomorrow morn.	
Victor	Nay, 'tis a foul mistake. The murderer	
	Is known to me; Justine is innocent.	

Enter ALPHONSE FRANKENSTEIN.

Alphonse	Long hop'd-for Victor, come home finally!	
Victor	Dear sir, would the conditions were less bleak.	135

Alphonse	Thou camest; 'tis the only thing that matters.

[They shake hands.

Ernest	By heaven, Papa, Victor doth report	
	He knoweth who hath slain our William small.	
Alphonse	Alas, we do. I rather had ne'er known	
	Th'identity of William's killer than	140
	To have discover'd such depravity	
	And base ingratitude in one methought	
	So loyal, true, and full of value.	
Victor	—Nay,	
	Dear father, thou art much mistaken, sir:	
	Justine is innocent.	
Alphonse	—Would she were so.	145
	Her trial shall commence by morning's light,	
	And gladly would I her acquittal see.	

Enter ELIZABETH LAVENZA.

Elizabeth	Here standeth one who bringeth with him hope,	
	Whose advent is a drink for hungry hearts.	
Victor	O, my Elizabeth!	

[They embrace.

Elizabeth	—Mayhap thou shalt	150
	Reveal some way to justify Justine,	
	Who must be guiltless of the horrid crime.	
	Indeed, who can be safe if she's condemn'd?	

	I set my faith upon her innocence	
	As if it were mine own. This double woe	155
	Is far too great a load for us to lift.	
	If she, whom I do trust, convicted is,	
	Ne'er shall I know of happiness again.	

Victor   That she is innocent will soon be prov'd.
             Fear not; let mine assurance cheer your spirit.   160

Elizabeth   How kind thou art, for all believe her guilt,
             Which hath these many days dejected me.

Ernest   Yet all the evidence doth point to her.

Alphonse   Despite what we may wish, truth cannot hide.

Elizabeth   To see those whom I love convinc'd so soon   165
             Hath left me wholly hopeless.

Alphonse   —Cherish'd niece,
             Be not disconsolate. If, as thou think'st,
             Justine is innocent, thou mayst rely
             Upon the justice of Genevan laws,
             Which shall decide the matter sans a shadow   170
             Of partiality.

Victor   —Come, let's within.
             More of this case shall we discuss anon
             And learn how, from despair, hope may be drawn.

                                                        [Exeunt.

SCENE 2.
Geneva. A courtroom.

Enter JUSTINE MORITZ.

Justine	Let me have calm, though calm is far from me.	
	This morning I present myself before	
	The court that doth accuse me dreadfully.	
	Yet how shall I defend myself when I	
	But little know the truth I should uphold?	5

Enter VICTOR FRANKENSTEIN, ELIZABETH LAVENZA, ALPHONSE FRANKENSTEIN, ERNEST FRANKENSTEIN, MAGISTRATE, OFFICER, a JURY OF CITIZENS, and many OTHER CITIZENS.

Magistrate	The case of Justine Moritz shall be heard,	
	Who stands accus'd within our righteous court	
	Of murdering young William Frankenstein.	
	Those who are witnesses, pray stand and speak.	
Citizen 1	Your honor, many thanks. This lass Justine	10
	Was with the young lad, William, on the day	
	Of which she is accus'd. The two did run	
	Across my field toward the river, sir.	
Magistrate	Seem'd they unhappy?	
Citizen 1	—Such I could not tell.	
Alphonse	[*aside:*] 'Tis not conclusive, not by any means.	15
Citizen 2	That day, I search'd the ground for fishing worms,	
	And heard the poor lad shrieking piercingly,	
	As if he fear'd some looming mortal threat.	

	It took some moments, ere I certain was—	
	Methought perchance 'twas but mine ear's odd	
	trick—	20
	Once sure, I thither ran with utmost speed,	
	But—rue the day—I haply tripp'd and fell.	
Elizabeth	[*aside:*] O curse the clod of earth that caus'd the fall.	
Citizen 2	When I, at last arriv'd unto the scene,	
	The boy had long been silent, and his screams	25
	Had, like a tree branch, been cut swiftly off.	
	I stood far off for fear of the unknown,	
	And spied the lady near the riverbank.	
	There—hid by bushes—I did see her kneel	
	In some confusion o'er the boy's dead corpse.	30
	It seem'd to me she did beweep her act.	
	No other living soul was near the two.	
Victor	[*aside:*] No living soul, how accurate the words—	
	He who slay'd William lives unnat'rally.	
Officer	When we did apprehend the suspect, sir,	35
	She had the costly locket in her pouch.	
	'Tis known the boy had ask'd his cousin for 't.	
	Our just conclusion is that Justine Moritz—	
	In action either plann'd or unrehears'd—	
	Did take the locket and the miniature,	40
	Purloining it most forcef'lly from the boy.	
	When he did yell to stop her heinous crime,	
	She strangl'd him by strength of her two hands.	
Ernest	[*aside:*] Description terrible, and all too clear.	
Magistrate	These witnesses have shar'd their testimony.	45
	Thou, lass, what wouldst thou say in thy defense?	

Justine	God knoweth of mine innocence entire,
	Yet I shall not pretend you shall acquit
	Me on the strength of protestations mere.
	I hope the character I've ever borne 50
	Inclines your wise interpretation to
	My favor, though the fateful circumstance
	Appeareth doubtful and suspicious both.
	As for the locket and the miniature
	Appearing on my person, I confess 55
	I have no power of explaining it.
	'Tis only in conjecture's realm that I
	May ponder on the probabilities.
	I have no enemy upon the earth,
	And surely none could be so wickèd as 60
	To wantonly destroy me. I commit
	My cause unto the justice of my judges,
	Yet see but little cause whereon to hope.
	I beg permission that a witness may
	Examin'd be upon the subject of 65
	My character. And if their words shall not
	Outweigh the scale of my supposèd guilt,
	I stand before ye as a lass condemn'd,
	Though I would pledge my soul's salvation on
	The truth and honor of mine innocence. 70
Victor	[*aside:*] Most noble speech from woman so belied.
Magistrate	If one would rise to speak for the accus'd,
	Let them be known.

[The courtroom is silent for a moment.

Elizabeth	—In conscience, I must stand.
	I am the cousin of th'unhappy child

Who was torn down by murder most unkind— 75
In troth, more like a sister, living with
His parents since before the lad was born.
Mayhap to speak on this occasion shall
Seem most indecent, but I cannot see
My fellow creature bound to perish through 80
The cowardice of her pretended friends;
I must reveal her character to you.
For two years have I liv'd with the accus'd,
Who ever was the most benevolent,
Agreeable of people. She stood fast— 85
With the persistence of Penelope—
As Madame Frankenstein, my darling aunt,
Did perish from her illness ultimate,
And this Justine did nurse her all the while.
Not long thereafter did she tend her own 90
Sick mother, for which act we all admir'd her.
She was a second mother to this boy—
E'en William, whom we lov'd devotedly.
Despite the evidence that you have heard,
I have faith in her perfect innocence. 95
She no temptation had toward the deed.
And as for that small bauble—which is thought
To be her motive for the shocking crime,
And is the point on which the chief proof rests—
Had she so earnestly desir'd the piece, 100
I would have willingly made it her gift,
So much do I esteem and value her.

Magistrate The witnesses have spoken, and the court
Shall render its swift judgment in the case.
Pray, officer, escort the lady hence. 105

[Exeunt Justine, magistrate, officer, and jury.

Citizen 3	[*to citizen 4:*] The lass is guilty, sure as sun doth rise.
Citizen 4	Methinks that her adopted family Hath, sadly, been deceiv'd by her dissembling.
Citizen 3	Forsooth, the lure of riches often tempts The honest into waywardness and crime. 110
Citizen 4	'Tis likely she'll be hang'd ere evening comes.
Victor	[*aside:*] Is't possible the public voice doth turn So suddenly against our poor Justine? It seems the demon hath, in one fell swoop, Play'd sport with my dear brother's being whilst 115 Betraying innocence to shame and death. Where once I saw a glimmer of faint hope, Now I do fear the worst shall come to pass.

All wait. Enter JUSTINE MORITZ, MAGISTRATE, OFFICER, and a JURY OF CITIZENS.

Alphonse	So soon return'd?
Ernest	—Perhaps they were convinc'd By what our brave Elizabeth declar'd. 120
Elizabeth	Alas, I dread the opposite.
Magistrate	—Hear ye: The case of Justine Moritz is resolv'd. Upon a further revelation were The ballots cast in unanimity.
Victor	[*aside:*] "A further revelation"—what means this? 125

Magistrate	This Justine Moritz is found guilty of
	The murder vile of William Frankenstein.
	She shall receive her death by hangman's noose.
	May God have mercy on her sinful soul,
	Though she but little mercy could afford 130
	Toward the tragic boy she cruelly kill'd.

Elizabeth   Justine! Nay, nay, it cannot be!

Victor   [*to magistrate:*]   —My lord,
What was the revelation that arose?
Is it some matter with the locket, sir?

Magistrate	That evidence we hardly did require 135
	In such a case, so glaring and so clear.
	Indeed, I'm glad of it—a jury is
	Not pleas'd to doom a criminal to death
	On circumstantial evidence alone,
	No matter how decisive it may be. 140
	The revelation, though, of which I spoke
	Is this: the very moment we repair'd
	Unto my chambers did the lass confess.

Ernest   Confess?

Magistrate	—Confess, to ev'ry charge she fac'd.
	Now, citizens, I bid ye leave the court, 145
	For swiftly must the wheels of justice turn.
	The family may bid the lass farewell.
	Then, officer, convey her to the jail.

[Exeunt magistrate, jury, and other citizens. Elizabeth approaches Justine.

Elizabeth   Justine, how can this be? Why didst thou take

| | My final consolation in this world? 150
| | Upon thine innocence I did rely,
| | And though I then was wretchèd utterly,
| | I was not mis'rable as I am now.

[Justine kneels before Elizabeth.

Justine   Wilt thou, Elizabeth, believe me wickèd,
             And join the chorus of mine enemies 155
             Who would condemn me as a murderer?

Elizabeth   Say wherefore kneelest thou if thou art guiltless?
             Ne'er have I been thine enemy, Justine—
             Not even with the evidence display'd—
             Until I heard thou didst declare thy guilt. 160
             'Tis naught but thy confession shakes my trust.

Justine   I did confess, but I confess'd a lie
             That I might absolution yet obtain.
             Now, though, the falsehood weighs more heavily
             Than any sin of which I was accus'd. 165
             The moment we walk'd through the courtroom door,
             The priest within—believing me to be
             No better than a monster—sieg'd me with
             Such threats of excommunication harsh
             And visions of perdition and hell's flames, 170
             That I subscrib'd unto the sordid lie.
             Methought, Elizabeth, thou wouldst believe—
             Thou who hast ever been my strength and stay.

Elizabeth   Justine, forgive me for my brief mistrust.
             I must proclaim thine innocence again 175
             And make the magistrate grant thee reprieve!

Justine   Nay, cousin, sister, friend, I will not have 't.

	No fear have I of death. That pang is past,
	And heav'n hath fit me with the courage to
	Endure the worst. A sad and bitter world 180
	I leave behind. I am resign'd to fate.
Victor	Thou art a wonder, and thine innocence
	Was ne'er in question in mine eyes, Justine.
	Indeed, when first I heard thou hadst confess'd,
	'Twas unbelievable unto my mind. 185
Justine	My humble thanks. In these, my final hours,
	Sincerest gratitude doth fill my heart
	For those who have their kindness shown to me.
	I draw nigh to my death most peacefully
	In knowing you, Elizabeth and Victor, 190
	Acknowledge and accept mine innocence.
Elizabeth	Would I could die with thee. I cannot live
	Within this world replete with misery.
Justine	Farewell, my dear Elizabeth, farewell
	Belovèd friend. And may this be the last 195
	Misfortune that thou ever sufferest.

[Exeunt.

Enter ROBERT WALTON as Chorus.

Robert	Justine did perish as a murderer,
	Her youthful neck stretch'd taut on scaffold bare.
	She left her friends bereft of ev'ry hope,
	And led the troubl'd Victor Frankenstein 200
	To grave considerations of his faults.

[Exit.

Enter VICTOR FRANKENSTEIN.

Victor	My anguis'd heart is set upon the rack	
	And tortur'd to th'extreme of human sense.	
	The voiceless grief of mine Elizabeth,	
	The boundless limits of my father's woe,	205
	The desolation of my smiling home—	
	All is the work of mine accursèd hands!	

Enter ELIZABETH LAVENZA.

Dear cousin, though I know the answer well,
How is it with thy spirit?

Elizabeth   —Victor, dear,
When I reflect upon the awful death   210
Of Justine Moritz, then are mine eyes chang'd:
No more see I the world and all its works
As formerly they did, to me, appear.
Ere now, I heard accounts of wrong and vice,
And they were as remote as fantasy.   215
At present, misery hath homeward come,
And folk appear as monsters in my mind,
Who do but thirst for one another's blood.
When falsehood can be spoken as the truth,
Who can assure themselves of happiness?   220
It seems I walk upon a precipice,
And thousands wait to push me in th'abyss.
Both William and Justine have gone to death,
Whilst somewhere hath a murderer escap'd.

Victor   [*aside:*] Alack, I fear the murd'rer is myself!   225

Elizabeth   Thy countenance, my darling, changeth so!

	Pray, calm thyself, for in thine aspect I	
	Espy expressions of despair and vengeance,	
	Which cause my soul to tremble horribly.	
	I prithee, banish all thy passions dark,	230
	Remembering the friends surrounding thee,	
	Who place our hopes on thee and wish for naught	
	But thy contentment and thy future health.	
	What more can possibly disturb our peace?	
Victor	Forgive me, generous Elizabeth.	235
	Thy reassurance cannot penetrate	
	The clouds of gray that hang about my mien.	
	Such ghastly weather deep within my mind	
	Must yet resolve itself into a squall	
	Ere I can wholly be restor'd to thee.	240
	The mists of mine own faults I must reform,	
	And shall find thee once I pass through the storm.	

[Exeunt.

SCENE 3.

Geneva. A mountainside.

Enter THE MONSTER.

Monster	The death of that impertinent young boy	
	Is but a prologue to the acts to come.	
	O hateful day when I receiv'd my life—	
	Why did this Frankenstein create a thing	
	That even he would turn from in disgust?	5
	I'll have my due or have my vengeance—both	
	Would bring me satisfaction in the height.	
	The man shall grant me life or taste more death.	
	No more of talking; time for action 'tis.	
	It is the wont of my creator to	10

          Go daily walking on the snowy hills.
          Today shall I encounter him at last,
          And bid him give me that which I am ow'd.
          A-ha! He comes—the hare toward the trap.

          He hides. Enter VICTOR FRANKENSTEIN.

Victor   Ye wand'ring spirits, if indeed ye wander,   15
          And rest not in your earthy, narrow beds,
          Allow me this faint happiness today—
          The pleasure of this moment pastoral—
          Or take me shortly, as your newfound friend,
          Away from ev'ry joy and pang of life.   20

                              [The monster steps forward.

Monster   At last, the time arriveth when we meet.

Victor   O, devil! Dost thou dare approach me here?
          Dost thou not fear the vengeance of mine arm,
          Which gladly I would wreak upon thy pate?
          Be gone, vile insect, ere I trample thee!   25
          Would that I could—with the extinction of
          Thy terrible existence—once again
          Restore those victims whom thou murderèdst!

Monster   'Tis this reception—fill'd with vehemence—
          I long expected. All despise the wretchèd,   30
          Thus must I hated be, who am, in truth,
          Most miserable of all living things.
          Thou—my creator, who didst give me life—
          Hast turn'd thy purpose unto killing me.
          How darest thou to make such sport of life?   35
          Do thou thy rightful duty unto me,
          And I shall do to thee—and humans all—

	What I owe in return. 'Tis simple, man:	
	Comply with my conditions, and I shall	
	Leave them and thee at peace forevermore.	40
	But if thou shouldst refuse, pray take thou heed:	
	I'll gladly glut the gaping maw of death,	
	Until 'tis satiated with the blood	
	Of thee and all thy friends who do remain.	
Victor	Abhorrèd monster, fiend from Satan sent!	45
	Hell's tortures are too merciful for thee.	
	Lay on, and I'll extinguish that rank spark	
	That negligently I bestow'd on thee!	

[*Victor tries to attack the monster, but the monster dodges and Victor falls to the ground.*

Monster	Thou shouldst give ear before thy hatred spendst.	
	Have I not suffer'd plentif'lly enow,	50
	That thou wouldst but increase my misery?	
	Though life is naught but anguish swelling e'er,	
	'Tis yet a precious gift, which I'll defend.	
	O Frankenstein, be unto others not	
	A man of virtue and upstanding deeds,	55
	Whilst thou dost shun the one thou owest justice	
	And clemency—belike affection, too.	
	Remember that I am thy handiwork;	
	I ought to be thine Adam, rather than	
	The fallen angel whom thou seek'st to crush.	60
	Around me ev'rywhere I witness bliss,	
	From which I solely am prohibited.	
	Once was I both benevolent and good;	
	'Tis suffering hath turn'd me to a fiend.	
	Make me but glad, and I'll be virtuous.	65
Victor	I will not hear thee. No community	

	Can there exist betwixt thee and myself.	
	We are and ever shall be enemies.	
	Depart, or we must fight unto the death.	

Monster   What words will move thy too-distemper'd heart?   70
             Will no entreaty turn thine eyes to me
             With favor—I, thy creature, who implore
             Thy goodness and compassion to appear?
             Completely banish'd from humanity,
             This icy landscape hath become my home,   75
             The deserts and the glaciers shelter me.
             By human law, the guilty are allow'd
             To speak their own defense ere they're condemn'd.
             Wilt thou not hear me ere thou callest me
             A murderer?

Victor   —Why mak'st thou me recall   80
             The circumstances which I shudder at,
             Of which I am the origin and author?
             Curs'd be the day when first thou light beheldst!
             Curs'd be the hands that form'd thee, even mine!

Monster   Hear yet my tale, which is both long and strange— 85
             Unto my mountain hut, pray follow thou.

Victor   [*aside:*] My curiosity doth urge me on,
             Compassion doth confirm my resolution.
             I, hitherto, assum'd 'twas he who slay'd
             My brother William, and would know for sure.   90
             Thus shall I fain comply with his demand,
             And hear the tale this woeful beast would tell.

                    Enter ROBERT WALTON as Chorus.

Robert   Creator and creation both repair'd

	Unto the monster's humble dwelling place.	
	Therein did Frankenstein hear ev'rything:	95
	The monster's disappearance to the wood,	
	How he did learn De Lacey's language well,	
	The scraps of paper left within his robe	
	Describing the profound experiment	
	And giving Victor's name and residence.	100
	The tale he told unto the moment when	
	He slaughter'd William and entrapp'd Justine.	

[Exit Walton.

Monster   The locket had I seen upon the boy,
          And mark'd it as I wrung the life from him.
          I thought, at first, to wake the sleeping girl   105
          With taunting words: "Behold thy paramour,
          Who would but give his life thy love t'obtain!
          Awake at once, belovèd mine, awake!"
          Yet, swiftly did I turn these thoughts away,
          She'd soon denounce me as a murderer.   110
          Instead, she would atone for my misdeeds—
          I bent and plac'd the locket in her pouch.

Victor   Thou villain! O, our poor, malign'd Justine!

Monster   Some days I wander'd in the area,
          And watch'd as thou return'dst from Ingolstadt.   115
          The trial I bore witness to with glee
          And did not mourn the lady when she hung.

Victor   Enow! I've done with thee. Get hence, thou brute!

Monster   Nay, we'll not part till thou dost gratify
          My requisition: I am too alone,   120
          And not a human will make peace with me.

	Yet one who is deform'd and horrible	
	As I would ne'er deny herself to me.	
	My true companion must be fashion'd from	
	My selfsame species, with the same defects.	125
	It is thy task this being to create.	
Victor	Foh! Not for the wide world. I do refuse.	
	No torture thou nor any could devise	
	Shall e'er extort my mind's or soul's consent.	
	Thou mayst make me most mis'rable, indeed,	130
	Yet ne'er make me so base in mine own eyes.	
	Should I create another like thyself,	
	Joint wickedness could desolate the world.	
Monster	I'll torture not, but reason with thee plainly.	
	Shall I respect one who condemneth me?	135
	Nay, I'll not bend 'neath abject slavery;	
	As thou wouldst, I'll revenge mine injuries.	
	If I cannot inspire love, I'll cause fear—	
	And chiefly unto thee, mine enemy.	
	Not harm thy body, nay, I'll crush thy heart.	140
	What I do ask is reas'nable enow:	
	A creature of another sex who is	
	As hideous and twisted as myself.	
	We monsters, then, shall separate ourselves	
	And live far from the press of human life.	145
	I pray, do not deny me my request.	
Victor	[*aside:*] Alas, there's justice in his argument.	
	[*To monster:*] But how will you, in exile, persevere?	
	You will return, your passions leading on,	
	And double shall be your destruction then.	150
	Thou swearest thou shalt harmless prove, and yet	
	Hast thou not malice shown to such degree	
	That I should never trust thee? Is this not	

| | Some feint with which thy triumph to increase, |
| | Affording thy grave vengeance wider scope? 155 |

Monster   I'll not be trifl'd with. Thou must respond.
           My vices are but children rank of the
           Enforcèd solitude that I abhor.
           My virtues shall arise when I, at last,
           Live in communion with my equal half. 160

Victor   [*aside:*] Heav'n help me, but the monster doth persuade.
           Would I feel any diff'rent in his place?
           The scorn humanity has plac'd on him—
           Which started with my own desertion cruel—
           Has led him unto acts of hate profound. 165
           'Twould not be thus had he a better start,
           Or someone to regard him with fresh eyne.
           [*To monster:*] I do consent unto thy just demand,
           Upon thy solemn oath that thou shalt leave
           The continent of Europe evermore. 170
           If thou wilt live beyond where humans dwell,
           I shall create a complement for thee,
           A female who shall into exile follow.

Monster   I swear, by sun and blue of sky in heav'n,
           By that Promethean fire inside my core, 175
           If thou dost grant my wish, no human shall
           Behold my sad, deformèd face again.
           Depart, then, Frankenstein, unto thy home,
           Commence thy labors. I shall watch thee well.

           [Exit monster. Victor weeps.

Victor   O stars and clouds and winds, you'll mock me so. 180
           If ye do pity me, take ev'ry sense

And memory from me. If ye shall not,
Leave me in darkness and depart from me.
Forthwith I'll to my family again.
I love them past all measure, sum, or bound.   185
To save them, I shall wholly dedicate
Myself unto the duty I do hate.

[Exit.

SCENE 4.

Geneva. The Frankenstein household.

Enter ALPHONSE FRANKENSTEIN.

Alphonse My faithful wife hath her eternal rest,
Her youngest son is lost to me fore'er,
His murd'rer—once a trusted friend—hath hang'd.
Too much of death accompanies my age,
Too vast the unexpected tragedies.   5
'Tis wrong when one too early mourns a spouse,
When life together proveth passing sweet.
'Tis wrong for someone to outlive their child,
Which doth, methinks, upset the nat'ral order.
'Tis wrong when one would take another's life,   10
Which is a sin against e'en heav'n itself.
'Tis all too much, too much. More I'd not bear.
Mine only consolation is that I
Still have mine Ernest and Elizabeth,
And that my Victor doth begin to heal   15
From all those miseries he lately fac'd.
Mayhap a season made for healing comes—
Past is our time to mourn; 'tis time to dance.

Enter VICTOR FRANKENSTEIN.

Victor	Holla, sir.	
Alphonse	—Victor, thou art well met, son.	
	I gladly note—and pleas'd am—thou resum'st	20
	Thy former pleasures and seem'st more thyself.	
	Yet still it seems thou shunn'st our company.	
	I would find out the cause of this effect,	
	Or rather say, the cause of this defect,	
	For this effect defective comes by cause.	25
	In setting all my thoughts unto the matter,	
	One answer struck me, which I'd put to thee.	
Victor	[*aside:*] How well did I attempt to hide the truth—	
	Is my dilemma somehow known to him?	
Alphonse	Long have I forward look'd with hope upon	30
	That day when thou wilt wed Elizabeth.	
	The two of ye since childhood were attach'd,	
	And always have seem'd suited to each other.	
	Perchance, though, I am blind unto the truth:	
	Mayhap thou dost as sister look on her,	35
	Yet have no wish to take her as thy wife.	
	Perhaps thou hast another paramour,	
	Though on Elizabeth thy die was cast.	
	Is't possible such matters trouble thee?	
Victor	Dear father, let me rest thine ev'ry qualm:	40
	I love my cousin tenderly, sincerely,	
	And ne'er another woman did espy	
	Who so completely doth claim mine esteem.	
	My future hopes and prospects fully are	
	Bound in the expectation of our union.	45

Alphonse	Thy reassurance giveth me more joy
	Than I have, far too long, experienc'd.
	The warmth betwixt the two of you shall light
	The dreary gloom of recent days away.
	O, wherefore shall we not thy wedding rush— 50
	Move forward with the long-awaited date—
	That in the early celebration of
	Your nuptials, we'll banish darkness quite?
Victor	[*aside:*] The thought fills me with horror and dismay!
	Though I am bound unto my darling lass, 55
	And fain would start life with Elizabeth,
	What should the monster make of this event?
	What miseries shall he wreak on we two,
	If I my solemn contract with him break
	Or find myself unequal to the task? 60
	I'll undertake a journey that shall both
	Delay our wedding day, and give me time
	The dreaded, promis'd creature to produce.
	[*To Alphonse:*] O father, there is naught I more desire
	Than to be husband to Elizabeth. 65
	Yet, for my spirit, which, as thou dost know,
	As lately unto melancholy turn'd,
	'Twould be a boon to journey for some time.
Alphonse	Where wouldst thou go?
Victor	—To England, sir, with haste.
	Let me fly thither for a length of time, 70
	Where I shall find, once more, my former strength.
	Then eagerly I'll to Geneva come
	And marry my belov'd Elizabeth.

Alphonse	If thou dost wish it, take my blessing full.
	It doth delight me, seeing thee enthus'd 75
	For such a venture.
Victor	—Then is it resolv'd.
Alphonse	One matter else: take Clerval thither.
Victor	—Why?
	[*Aside:*] Though Henry is my most devoted friend,
	To work will hopeless prove if he is nigh.
Alphonse	In Ingolstadt, thine isolation grew 80
	Unhealthy, nearly cost thy very life.
	I prithee, let thy friend go with thee, son—
	Much comfort shall it give me, verily.
Victor	It shall be as thou sayest, father.
Alphonse	—Well!
	Thou hast appeas'd an old man's feeble mind. 85
Victor	Nay, not a whit. Thou art still young enow.
Alphonse	May peace go with thee unto England, Victor.
	Our blessing for thy journey we afford,
	With hopes thou shalt hereafter be restor'd.

[Exeunt.

SCENE 5.
Geneva.

Enter ELIZABETH LAVENZA.

Elizabeth	What is my purpose in a hurting world?	
	When illness runneth rampant through the house,	
	When justice is by missteps overthrown,	
	When foes are threatening the commonweal,	
	When all the planet hath been lit aflame,	5
	When miseries and pressures gather round	
	Like flies unto a carcass long since dead,	
	What helpful light is mine to volunteer?	
	The toll of tragedy hath call'd on us—	
	We are no strangers unto suffering—	10
	Yet still I question how I should respond.	
	I cannot, like a boastful politician,	
	Proclaim that all, in time, shall turn to good.	
	I cannot, like a person steep'd in wealth,	
	Use capital to guard 'gainst further woe.	15
	I cannot ply the trade of medicine,	
	That I might inj'ry heal or sickness cure.	
	I cannot, like an artist or a bard,	
	Distract the populace with pleasant pastimes.	
	Instead, I shall employ the strengths I have:	20
	Speak out when I observe injustices,	
	Tend unto those whose souls are weariest,	
	Prove best of friends e'en in foul weather's gloom,	
	And nurture those whom fate hath given me.	

Enter VICTOR FRANKENSTEIN.

Victor	Holla, Elizabeth, dear cousin kind.	25
	Thy visage, I perceive, resembleth one	
	Who standeth on the bow of vessel grand	

	And looks toward the destination far,	
	Ne'er noticing the waves that bat the ship.	
Elizabeth	'Tis true, my thoughts are many miles away.	30
Victor	Would that I could peruse the pages of	
	The book thou writest deep within thy mind.	
Elizabeth	Though I am author of a tome confus'd—	
	Unworthy for a reader such as thou—	
	Each word I'll gladly share.	
Victor	—Elizabeth,	35
	I come with news.	
Elizabeth	—Not more of tragedy?	
Victor	Nay. I fear disappointment is my theme.	
Elizabeth	Say on.	
Victor	—Before I speak the matter whole,	
	I prithee hear thou me: I thee adore.	
	Thou art the cornerstone on which I'll build	40
	The edifice of all my years to come.	
Elizabeth	Belike a load too heavy for this pebble.	
Victor	Nay, thou art such a sure and steadfast rock	
	Would make Gibraltar green with jealousy.	
Elizabeth	Thy loving words I do appreciate,	45
	Yet cease not my unease o'er what thou'lt tell.	
	Thine adultation ere thou disappoint'st	
	Is like dessert before the toothache comes.	
	More matter, with less art. What is thy news?	

Victor	To cure my melancholy, troubl'd mind,	50	
	My father hath giv'n leave—with Henry there		
	To save me from the solitary life—		
	To travel unto England presently.		

Victor To cure my melancholy, troubl'd mind, 50
My father hath giv'n leave—with Henry there
To save me from the solitary life—
To travel unto England presently.

Elizabeth [*aside:*] A further separation and delay
Of that sweet union for which I do hope. 55
Alas, how can I bear to say farewell,
When lately we have borne such misery?
'Tis here that I must set myself aside,
Not selfish be, but prove a loving friend.
[*To Victor:*] If thou believ'st the trip shall do thee well, 60
I'll not gainsay thy words, thy plans, thy will.
Instead, as one who waiteth through the night
In fervent expectation of the dawn,
I shall endure the time.

Victor —Elizabeth!
Thou art a paragon of steadfastness, 70
Who giveth me more grace than I have earn'd.

Elizabeth The one who earneth grace ne'er knows its pow'r.

Victor The one who knoweth love e'er feels its warmth.

Elizabeth I shudder when I think thou shalt endure
Continued suffering when thou art gone, 75
The inroads of thy misery and grief
Through which thy soul must valiantly advance
Ere thou art fully mended in the end.
'Tis excellent that Henry shall attend—
He hath prov'd better than a friend before 80
And shall again, as thou dost bravely face

	The dark night of the soul. Make haste, sweet man,	
	That those who love you may see thee again	
	Before we've time for worry, doubt, or fear.	
Victor	'Twill be as fast as fire consumeth fuel,	85
	Then shall we reunited be.	
Elizabeth	—Farewell.	
	The word, methinks, is too oft in my mouth,	
	Yet once more do I offer it to thee.	

[Exit Elizabeth.

Victor	All is decided, with the hardest deed—	
	To tell Elizabeth that I must leave—	90
	At last accomplish'd. I'll to England next,	
	And there devise some separation from	
	Kind Henry, that my work may yet proceed.	
	The separation from Geneva shall	
	Protect my family unfortunate,	95
	In keeping that foul phantom far from them.	
	Although from danger they shall, then, be safe,	
	An agitation vast doth gnaw at me.	
	My nerves do rattle at the coming toil,	
	Which taketh me beyond my native soil.	100

[Exit.

SCENE 1.
Orkney.

Enter VILLAGERS 1 and 2.

Villager 1	Whar's that?	
Villager 2	—Ho, Michael. 'Tis but Helga, lad.	
Villager 1	Ach, Helga, lass, well met. Whence hiv ye come?	
Villager 2	Doon Finstown way, tae gather groatie buckies.	
Villager 1	And found ye any of the peedie shells?	
Villager 2	Aye, one apiece for each o' me three bairns.	5
Villager 1	Beuy, beuy! The day is blashy. Are ye drookid?	
Villager 2	As drookid as a neep still in the gutter. Still, Michael, you'll nae find me pleepan boot it. To bide in Orkney, with its kye and hooses, To blether with your freends, all in the grimleens— The ferry-loopers ne'er such pleasures ken.	10
Villager 1	Troth, Helga. When the day for punding come Oot on North Ronaldsay, and hunder folk Come roond to caa the sheep atween the punds, Me heart grows muckle—canna ask for more.	15
Villager 2	Aye. Will ye walk?	
Villager 1	—Nae bother. After ye.	

[Exeunt.

Enter VICTOR FRANKENSTEIN and HENRY CLERVAL.

Henry	A journey to revive the human soul,	
	A friend with which to share th'experience—	
	This, truly, is how living was intended,	
	To claim the joy existence proffereth.	20
Victor	Would I could see with thine accepting eyes—	
	All I behold is sea most turbulent	
	And barren soil most rugged and unkind.	
	The landscape desolate doth offer a	
	Monotonous yet ever-changing scene,	25
	Rude waves that roar and dash on craggy shore.	
Henry	Thou must but fresh perspective cultivate.	
	Soon shalt thou be as merry as myself.	
Victor	Methinks a team of fools who ply their mimes,	
	Or players in a ribald comedy,	30
	Or fools with jests as sharp as poniard's points	
	Could ne'er make me as merry as thou art.	
	For mirth thou wert made, Henry, by my troth.	
Henry	O Victor, wilt thou not let me remain?	
Victor	Nay, nay. Enjoy thyself most heartily,	35
	And this shall, later, be our rendezvous.	
	Some month or two I may be occupied—	
	Pray interfere not in the interim;	
	Let me have peace and solitude awhile.	
	When I return, a lighter heart I'll have,	40
	Congenial to thine own happiness.	
Henry	In faith, I'd rather pass the days with thee,	
	Wheree'er thy solitary rambles go,	
	Than 'mongst these people, whom I little know.	
	Make haste, dear friend—repair, restore, return—	45
	That I may somewhat feel at home again,	
	Which is impossible when thou art absent.	

[They shake hands. Exit Henry. Victor walks to his lodging, where his laboratory equipment is set up.]

Victor   Now to my squalid hut. Unplaster'd walls
          And unhing'd doors let in the constant rain.
          Ne'er have I work'd in such poor circumstances.   50
          My labor—though 'tis irksome in the height—
          Shall not surcease until it is complete.
          With Henry gone, immers'd in solitude,
          I'm well position'd for creation's toils.
          Yet nervous grows my restless spirit here: 55
          When first I did create the monster rank,
          Enthusiastic frenzy blinded me
          To ev'ry horror of the goal I chas'd.
          Now, though, my blood hath turn'd cold in my veins,
          My body sick at what my hands must do.   60
          I also fear my persecutor's wrath—
          'Tis possible he watcheth even now.
          Alas, I am hoist by mine own petard:
          My future pays the price for my bleak past.

[Exit.

He works. Enter ROBERT WALTON as Chorus.

Robert   A fortnight Frankenstein endeavor'd to   65
          Create a second being, as 'twas vow'd.
          When near complete, his senses did awake
          Unto the horrid possibilities.

[Exit Robert.

Enter VICTOR FRANKENSTEIN with an unfinished BODY upon his laboratory table.

Victor   Before, I did create a horrid fiend,
          Releasing evil pure upon the world.   70
          I have, almost, another being made—
          Delinquent conscience! O, how could I so?
          Endow'd with life, she may prove vile as he,

	Or some ten thousand times more wicked still!	
	Forfend me from creations such as these—	75
	Foul is the man who fashions fouler deeds,	
	Rank are the hands that render ranker crimes.	
	And what if she shall neither love her mate	
	Nor give assent unto the pact we've sworn?	
	Keep me from further injury, ye gods,	80
	Enwrap me in your virtue, that I may	
	Not replicate the sin of yesteryear,	
	Suppressing right to bargain with the devil.	
	Take ye my hands and use them righteously,	
	Extinguishing my baser instincts to	85
	Ignite bold flashes of refining fire.	
	Now, to 't—what I created, I'll destroy!	

In a rage, VICTOR destroys his equipment and the BODY. Enter THE MONSTER.

Monster	Thou fool! O'er thee have I watch'd constantly,	
	Ensuring thou wouldst keep our covenant.	
	Thou hast demolish'd all thy careful work!	90
	What is it thou intendst by such misdeeds?	
	Wouldst disregard thy promises to me?	
	I have endur'd much toil and misery—	
	Incalc'lable fatigue, and cold, and want—	
	In following thee cross fair Europe's hills.	95
	Wilt thou, when all is done, destroy my hopes?	
Victor	Begone! My promises are hereby void.	
	Ne'er will I make another like thyself,	
	Thine equal in deformity and malice.	
Monster	I reason'd with thee once, but thou hast prov'd	100
	Unworthy of my condescension, rogue.	
	Thou dost believe thyself dejected quite,	
	Yet 'tis within my pow'r to break thee, such	
	That light of day shall hateful be to thee.	
	Thou my creator art, yet I'm thy master!	105

Victor	Thy threats shall not move me to wickedness.	
	They, rather, do confirm my steadfast will	
	To keep thee from a partner to thy vice.	
	I'll not set loose upon the earth a sprite	
	Who doth delight in wretchedness and death.	110
	Away, thou imp—I'll no more speak with thee.	
	Thy words shall but exasperate my rage.	
Monster	Thine hours shall pass in dread and misery,	
	And soon the bolt shall fall from yonder sky	
	That ravishes thy happiness fore'er.	115
	Revenge shall dearer be than light or food.	
	Beware, my fearlessness doth make me pow'rful.	
	Thou shalt repent of all the injuries	
	That thou upon the hapless dost inflict.	
Victor	Pray, poison not the air with further sound.	120
	My resolution did I plainly speak,	
	And shall not, like a coward, bend to thee.	
Monster	'Tis well, I go, but pray remember this:	
	I shall be with thee on thy wedding-night.	

[Exit.

Victor	O, would that I could pass my length of days	125
	Upon this rock, uninterrupted by	
	Whatever shocks of miseries may come.	
	Yet work remaineth, ere the morning comes—	
	I must dispose of that I did create,	
	Those body parts that human would appear	130
	To any who behold the sever'd limbs.	

[He picks up pieces of the body and puts them into a sack.
                Unto the harbor 'neath the moonlight's glow,
                Where I'll row out and drop the fetid load.
[He takes the sack to the harbor, where he gets into a boat and rows to sea.
                The fog and mist of night enclose me quite,
                To hide my shocking acts from peeping eyne.   135
                If any witnesses but knew the truth—
                No murderer dispensing of a corpse,

> But one protecting folk from greater ills—
> They would applaud mine exploits heartily.
> *[He dumps the body parts into the sea.*
> Back, now, unto the shore, and then to Henry,   140
> Whom I shall greet with such profound delight
> That he shall think me mad. Ha, let it be!
> To see his face, to see Elizabeth,
> Is all I further ask of this sad life.
> *[The wind blows harshly.*
> My rowing is disrupted by the wind—   145
> Where I would paddle closer to the shore,
> The squall doth carry me more distant yet.
> Now would I give a thousand lengths of sea
> For one small acre made of barren ground—
> The winds above be done! O, faulty boat,   150
> Which draws me outward, more and more remote!
>
> *[Exit.*

SCENE 2.

Ireland. A street. The next morning.

Enter KIRWIN, a magistrate, and three VILLAGERS.

Kirwin	What is the matter, gentles, that ye come
	Awaking me so early in the morn?
Villager 3	Beg pardon, magistrate, but you must hear:
	'Twas late last night—as I was fishing with
	My brother and my nephew—we espied 5
	A body of a man along the beach.
	At first, we thought him drown'd within the waves,
	Then toss'd upon the sand by raging wind,
	For, as you know, last night the gusts were wild.
Kirwin	Yea, sirrah. Pray, continue with your tale. 10
Villager 4	Examination of the body did
	Reveal our supposition for a lie:
	The clothes were dry, the skin not yet grown cold.

	Unto a cottage we convey'd him straight,	
	Yet could restore no signs of life thereto.	15
	No sign of violence did appear on him	
	Except the marks of fingers round his neck.	

Kirwin   A murder? Strangulation on our shores?

Villager 5 So doth it seem, yet there is more.

Kirwin   —Speak, then!

Villager 5 At dawn's light, something passing strange appear'd: 20
            Beyond the shoreline I beheld a boat,
            With but a single passenger within.

Kirwin   Do you suspect the killer was therein?

Villager 3 No other supposition could we make.

Kirwin   We must, then, find the boat.

Villager 4   —We have not done.   25
            The very vessel hath, of late, made landing,
            And he who was therein approacheth now!

Enter VICTOR FRANKENSTEIN.

Victor   Good friends, pray, can ye tell me where I am—
            What is this town? Where have I landfall made?

Villager 5 Thou shalt know soon enow. Belike thou hast   30
            Arriv'd within a place not to thy taste.
            And neither shalt thou be consulted as
            To what thy quarters shall be—this we'll judge.

Victor   Why have you answer'd me so rudely, sir?
            Methinks 'tis not the custom of the English   35
            To welcome strangers inhospitably.

Villager 5	Naught of the English custom do I know, Yet here, in Ireland, we do villains hate.
Victor	A villain? Wherefore use this epithet? Hath my small boat to Ireland taken me? 40
Villager 3	[*indicating Kirwin:*] Thou must, to this man, give account anon.
Victor	Why should I give account of mine own self? Is Ireland not a country free?
Villager 3	—Forsooth, 'Tis free enow for honest citizens. This man is Kirwin, local magistrate, 45 And thou must give accounting for the death Of one poor gentleman found murder'd here.
Kirwin	The evidence is most suggestive, sir, And as thou art a stranger in this land— Thine accent plain as nose upon thy face— 50 Thou verily art subject to our law. [*To villager 4:*] Where is the body, sirrah?
Villager 4	—In the cottage. Once we did know him dead, we mov'd him not.
Kirwin	Well reason'd. [*To Victor:*] Sir, I bid thee come withal. [*Aside to villagers:*] Let us behold him well, and we'll see what 55 Effect the sight produceth on his mien.

[They walk to a nearby cottage.

Enter VILLAGER 6, with a BODY upon the couch.

Villager 6	You are most welcome, magistrate. Come in— The body lieth there.
Kirwin	—Pray, sir, behold.

[Victor looks at the body and realizes it is Henry Clerval's body.

Victor Alack, my Henry! Fie, my dearest friend!
My murd'rous machinations have depriv'd 60
E'en thee of that one life thou liv'dst so well.
Two lives already have my deeds undone,
Whilst other prey awaiteth destiny.
But thou—my benefactor and my friend!
Why sink I not 'neath senselessness and rest? 65
Death snatches blooming children quickly hence,
Who once had been their parents' only hopes.
How many brides and youthful lovers were
One day in bloom of health, and on the next
Were but the food of worms in tomb's decay? 70
Of what material have I been wrought
To so resist the many thousand shocks
That flesh is heir to, which—like turning of
The wheel—my torture e'er reneweth? O!

[Victor faints.

Kirwin This fainting is, methinks, a sign of guilt, 75
Which hath the very air ta'en from his breast.
Mayhap a reckoning divine hath come,
Which drives the shameful criminal to swoon.
Convey him to a jail, where we shall wait
Until he doth regain his senses full. 80

[Exeunt Victor with villagers 3, 4, and 5, as they carry him to a jail cell. Kirwin leaves the cottage with villager 6.

Enter ALPHONSE FRANKENSTEIN.

Alphonse [*to Kirwin:*] Good sir, I was sent thither, you to seek.
My name is Alphonse Frankenstein. My son—
He Victor Frankenstein—is charg'd with crimes
That I can prove he was not party to.

Kirwin	Your swift appearance is a wonder, sir. The man was taken hence not long ago. How is it that you hither come so soon?	85
Alphonse	For weeks have I pursued my son with haste. He hath been ill of late, and went to England That he his former humors might restore. His friend accompanied him on the trek. This selfsame friend, young Clerval, hath sent word A fortnight past: mine errant son desir'd That they split ways just after reaching Orkney. They did so, although Clerval thought it rash— Thus did he write me. Straight I follow'd on, Concern'd for how my son might fare alone. 'Twas yesterday I reach'd the Orkney isles, But to discover I had miss'd him just. I took the morning crossing hitherward, And only now arriv'd and heard the news: My son accus'd of murdering a man Who, yesternight, was found upon the shore. 'Twas last night, though, my son did Orkney leave, And journey'd all the night upon the sea. He could not be the poor man's murderer. Alas, would Henry were but here to speak, He who doth know of Victor's latest days.	90 95 100 105
Kirwin	Your tale, sir, doth amaze. And who is Henry?	
Alphonse	He is the friend whereof I spoke.	
Kirwin	—Alas, Unhappy tidings I must render you: When your son saw the body, he did weep And call'd the dead one Henry all the while.	110
Alphonse	O, can it be? Shall heartbreak stike again? I beg you, sir: may I my Victor see?	115
Kirwin	[*to villager 6.*] Get thee unto the jailhouse presently And hither bring this Frankenstein, I pray.	

Villager 6	With all good speed, wise magistrate. This tale Would make a snake stand upright at attention.	

[Exit villager 6.

Alphonse	Do you have any children, magistrate?	120
Kirwin	Yea, three. A daughter and two sons have I.	
Alphonse	Well do you know the pain and joy that comes With parenting.	
Kirwin	—Indeed, I often jest The only scripture I am certain of Is that familiar tale of Cain and Abel. When they were young, my children fought an 'twere The Colosseum, they the gladiators. 'Twas only when they older, wiser grew, That they became fast friends who dwelt in peace.	125
Alphonse	My children were the opposite, in faith. As youth, they liv'd in happiness most rare— Few were the sharp words spoken in our home. 'Tis only now, when they are older, that The agony, distress, and pain arrive.	130

Enter VICTOR FRANKENSTEIN.

Victor	My father! Thou didst come. O, passing kind! Are you all safe? Elizabeth and Ernest?	135
Alphonse	Yea, let thy worried countenance be calm: All in Geneva carries on in peace, Whilst longing for thy safety and return. Thou travel'dst only to seek happiness, Yet some fatality pursueth thee. Poor Clerval—	140

Victor	—Woe and misery be mine! O Henry, longtime friend and loyal mate. My destiny hangs o'er me—like the sword That over Damocles unstably hung— Yet I must live, its ending to fulfill.	145
Kirwin	The presence of this syndic of Geneva Hath sav'd thee, Victor Frankenstein, from jail. We'll send our word to Orkney to confirm The details that thy father proffer'd me. Once settl'd 'tis, you both may take your leave. Sirs, I am truly sorry for your loss.	150

[Exit Kirwin.

Victor	My father, little dost thou know thy son. Justine—our most unhappy, poor Justine— Was as innocent as I, yet suffer'd she The selfsame charge for which I am suspected. She died for it, yet I'm the cause of all. Young William, pure Justine, devoted Henry, Died each one by the actions of my hands.	155
Alphonse	Nay, Victor, what infatuation's this? Thou speakest like a babe who talks and talks, But never with the sense of human speech. I do entreat thee, son ne'er make such bold Assertions like to these, or thou art ruin'd.	160
Victor	'Tis none of madness, father, I aver. The sun and heav'ns bear witness of my truth. These gentles died through mine own machinations. A thousand times I fain would shed my blood— Each drop a happiness—to save their lives, Yet I could not.	165
Alphonse	—No more, I prithee, son. Whilst we await the word that sets thee free, I'll offer thee a token of thy home:	170

	A letter from thy sweet Elizabeth,	
	Which, ere I left Geneva, she hath penn'd.	
Victor	Elizabeth! Her words I long for most.	175

[Alphonse hands Victor a letter, which Victor reads.

Enter ELIZABETH on balcony.

Elizabeth	Dear Victor—cousin, friend, and even more—	
	Thy father doth expect to bring thee home,	
	Which gives me hope I may see thee anon.	
	The winter, sans thy presence, dully passes.	
	When I behold thy countenance, I trust	180
	'Twill show both comfort and tranquility.	
	Yet what once made thee sad I fear still shall,	
	Its poor effect augmented by time's passage.	
	I dare no more postpone that which I have	
	Oft long'd to say e'en whilst thou absent wert.	185
	Our union from our infancy was plann'd—	
	So were we told we should with joy expect.	
	As children, were we two playfellows fast,	
	And valued friends as we became adults.	
	As siblings often may affection show	190
	Sans craving for a union intimate,	
	May not such also be the case with us?	
	Pray, tell me true: dost thou not love another?	
	My fear is that thou art, by honor, bound	
	To fill thy parents' wishes utterly,	195
	E'en if thine inclinations are oppos'd.	
	This reasoning is false. I do confess	
	I love thee, and e'er in my airy dreams	
	Thou art my constant friend and husband both.	
	Yet never would I make thee mis'rable	200
	Or unto thy desire place obstacles.	
	Give me thine answer when thou comest home.	
	When we do meet, if I do see but one	
	Sweet smile upon thy lips, 'twill be enow—	
	I need no other happiness than this.	205

	[Exit Elizabeth.	
Victor	[*aside:*] The lady's words ne'er cease to bring my tears.	
	Too long I've let her wonder at my will,	
	Like souls that wait in purgatory till	
	They are permitted through eternal gates.	
	Alas, but I recall the monster's words:	210
	"I shall be with thee on thy wedding-night."	
	Yet I'll not live in fear. Nay, nevermore—	
	The time hath come to stand and fight and live.	
	[*To Alphonse:*] Brave father, I am more than thankful for	
	The steady hand with which thou guidest me,	215
	Allowing not my deeds to bring despair	
	Upon thy true and gentle spirit. Come,	
	Soon shall my name be clear'd of any crime,	
	And then unto Geneva sans delay.	
Alphonse	My eldest boy, my treasure, my delight—	220
	Methinks our happiness is yet in sight.	

[Exeunt.

SCENE 3.
Geneva. The Frankenstein household.

Enter ELIZABETH LAVENZA.

Elizabeth	Word hath arriv'd from Ireland—farther e'en	
	Than we thought Victor's travels carried him—	
	Two letters that brought with them sparks of hope.	
	The first was brief, as father shar'd the news:	
	"Our Victor's well. We shall return anon."	5
	The second was in Victor's hand itself,	
	And brought such gladness to my waiting heart	
	That, as I read, my smile grew ever broader.	
	Although his words, in part, perturb'd my mind,	
	The sum of all the parts was bliss profound.	10
	Forsooth, my face did ache from being stretch'd	
	By all the unaccustom'd smiles it made.	

She reads the letter again. Enter VICTOR FRANKENSTEIN on balcony.

Victor	I fear, my most belovèd, cherish'd girl,	
	That little happiness remains for us.	
	Still, all the gladness I may yet enjoy	15
	Is center'd—unreservedly—in thee.	
	Pray, chase away thine idle fears, my love:	
	To thee alone I consecrate my life	
	And mine endeavors for contentment in 't.	
	I have one secret, dear Elizabeth—	20
	So awful it may chill thy frame with dread—	
	And when thou know'st it, thou shalt be surpris'd	
	That I survive what I have long endur'd.	
	This secret I'll unfold to thee, at length,	
	The very morning after we are wed.	25
	That joyous day cannot come fast enow—	
	We shall return, and soon thou'lt be my bride.	

[Exit Victor.

Elizabeth	Such words by his own hand, and all the house
	Expects him and our father presently.
	So many hours of waiting patiently 30
	Shall finally rewarded be. A-ha!

[She looks out of a window.

                Their carriage doth approach, they disembark!
                This advent is the zenith of my hopes!

Enter VICTOR FRANKENSTEIN and ALPHONSE FRANKENSTEIN.

Victor	Elizabeth, a balm to ev'ry sense:	
	For eyes, a lovely wonder to behold,	35
	For ears, the voice for which I so have long'd,	
	For smell, the waft of thine entrancing scent,	
	For taste, the hope of kisses yet to come,	
	For touch, the sweet embrace of love fulfill'd.	

[Victor and Elizabeth embrace.

Elizabeth	My Victor, home at last.

Victor	[*aside:*] —Her form doth tell	40
	A story of both anguish and concern:	
	How thin hath she become these many months,	
	How gaunt her visage from her worrying.	
	Still, though, that spark of life is burning bright,	
	Compassion ever blooming on her cheek—	45
	More fit companion for a gladder man.	
Elizabeth	Once thou hast rested, I have much to say.	
	Thy letter I receiv'd with earnest joy,	
	And hope our union may with haste arrive.	
Victor	Today, e'en now, upon the instant would	50
	I marry thee and call myself most bless'd.	
Alphonse	All preparations shall be made anon.	
	Elizabeth, pray fetch thou Ernest and	
	Tell all the house that Victor is return'd.	
Elizabeth	With joy, dear father.	

[Exit Elizabeth.

Alphonse	—Is thy heart resolv'd,	55
	With fix'd intent, upon thy wedding-day?	
	Of previous attachments thou hast none?	
Victor	Nay. I do wholly love Elizabeth,	
	And seeing her my judgment doth confirm.	
	Unearn'd and unforeseen delight is mine	60
	Upon the instant when we two are wed.	
	I prithee, let the day be set anon,	
	And gratefully I'll consecrate myself	
	Unto the happiness of her I love.	
Alphonse	'Tis true, misfortunes have befallen us,	65
	Thus let us cling the closer to the good,	
	And transfer love for those whom we have lost	
	To those who yet do live. Our circle shall	

	Be small, but bound by deep affection's ties	
	And mutual adversities we've known.	70
	When, finally, time softens thy despair,	
	Dear, newfound objects of our care shall come,	
	Replacing those of whom we were depriv'd.	

[Exeunt.

Enter CLERGY PERSON on balcony.

Clergy	Hear ye, as we proclaim the wedding banns	
	Of one Elizabeth Lavenza and	75
	Her Victor Frankenstein. If any know	
	A reason wherefore they should not be wed,	
	I bid ye be not silent, but come forth!	
	The happy wedding shall proceed apace.	

[Exit clergy person.

*Enter VICTOR FRANKENSTEIN and ELIZABETH LAVENZA,
now wed.*

Victor	My bride, is't possible art sorrowful?	80
	I would not have it. I have suffer'd much,	
	Belike more misery I shall endure—	
	Yet, for this day, let us enjoy the quiet	
	And freedom from despair our wedding brings.	
	Let us upon the fruits of marriage sup,	85
	And think not on whatever meals may come.	
Elizabeth	Yea, Victor, naught do I wish thee but joy,	
	That nothing shall distress thee e'er again.	
	If thou dost see concern upon my face,	
	I prithee know my heart is well contented.	90
	Some nagging voice tells me not to depend	
	Upon the prospect open 'fore us now,	
	Yet I shall heed no tone so sinister.	
	Today, unto the Alps we'll swiftly fly,	
	The wings of Mercury upon our backs,	95
	And Cupid's arrows guiding our way thither.	

	We shall observe the beauty of Mont Blanc,
	The clouds that rise around its massive dome,
	And, underneath, the lakes that shine like glass,
	Fill'd withal carefree fish innumerable 100
	And ev'ry pebble on the bottom clear
	Unto our eyes as planets in the heav'ns.
	The day is ours and bless'd by hand divine—
	How happy and serene all nature seems!

Victor [*aside:*] Though ev'ry step I take is fill'd with dread, 105
And I've my pistol and my dagger close
In case the beast should openly attack,
I must grant my Elizabeth her due
And join her hope that all the worst is pass'd.
[*To Elizabeth:*] O, best of wives and best of women
thou— 110
With thee beside me, naught shall rapture shake.

Elizabeth Today, at last, I have become thy bride,
Tonight, let us in love's embrace abide.

[Exeunt.

SCENE 1.
The Alps.

Enter THE MONSTER.

Monster   Across the mountains and across the sea,
My fury follows like a wolfhound keen.
With watchful eyes, I've track'd the newlyweds
From their reunion, joyful and unearn'd—
Their sweet embraces such as I'll ne'er know,   5
Her grasping him 'round his betraying neck
And kissing those dissembling, hateful lips—
Until their wedding on this very morn.
The happy day, when hope is at the height,
When from their misery they start to rest,   10
When ev'ry thought is of the future age
And gilded with the hue of heav'nly light,
Shall turn to ash and embers in a flash.
Most grooms recall their wedding readily,
And so shall this one, but with grief complete.   15
The bride, however: she shall not recall
This day in years to come, for she'll have none.
Belike 'tis mercy for the damsel, for
Should he be careless with his wedding vows
Like he was with the pledge he made to me,   20
She would have had a woeful married life.
Although my vile creator, Frankenstein,
Doth break the solemn oath he made to me,
My words to him I shall with glee fulfill:
"I shall be with thee on thy wedding-night"—   25
And here I am, my vengeance to exact.

He hides. Enter VICTOR FRANKENSTEIN and ELIZABETH LAVENZA.

Elizabeth   What is it that doth agitate thee, Victor?
            Thine anxiousness is writ upon thy face,
            Thine eyes flit yon and hither like a snipe,
            And ev'ry sound doth give thee such a fright   30
            That thou shalt leap forth from thy very skin.
            What is it thou dost fear?

Victor   —Peace, peace, my love.
            Should we but pass this night, all shall be safe,
            Yet I am rife with dread until the dawn.

Elizabeth   This terror pilfers love's rewards from thee.   35
            The night when we should claim our happiness,
            Thou art distracted by some threat unseen.
            Pray, come to bed and let us be one flesh.
            Full many years my heart has ach'd for thee—
            Let it not, on this night, be disappointed.   40

Victor   'Tis most unjust of me to make delay.
            I pray, Elizabeth, get thee to bed,
            And—after some few moments of inspection,
            In which I may our safety guarantee
            And reassure my most unsettl'd soul—   45
            I'll follow on with spirit most serene.

Elizabeth   Until thou comest, I shall rest in want.

[Exit Elizabeth into the bedroom. Exit the monster, unseen, following her.

Victor   Each moment I expect attack most sudden,
            The monster beating at the cottage door.
            I shall confirm the function of the locks,   50

	And verify each window is secur'd.	
	Perchance the monster shall not hither come,	
	And these inspections shall prove overcautious,	
	Mere wasted effort when my bride awaits.	
	Belike our wedding-night shall peaceful—	

Elizabeth   [*off stage, screaming:*]   —Aaaaaaah!   55

Victor   Alack, Elizabeth! What have I done?

Enter THE MONSTER, strangling ELIZABETH LAVENZA.

Monster   This is my gift upon thy wedding-night—
The recompense for her thou took'st from me!
[Elizabeth dies. The monster drops her body.
What cheer, my maker? Hast thou lost a friend?
Did I not give thee ample warning of   60
The consequences of denying me?

Victor   Thou monstrous, mangl'd, pox-mark'd canker-blossom!
[Victor pulls out a pistol to shoot the monster, who exits. Victor runs to Elizabeth's side.
O grief to grief increas'd sans sense or end—
As one by one, my friends are snatch'd away
To leave me desolate, alone, afeard.   65
Elizabeth, my cousin, friend, and bride!
Her bloodless arms, pale cheeks, and bruisèd neck,
Her form relax'd by death's eternal rest,
Her life pour'd out like water through a sieve—
Great God, take me as well! Why let me live?   70

[Exit.

SCENE 2.
Geneva.

Enter ALPHONSE FRANKENSTEIN and ERNEST FRANKENSTEIN.

Alphonse	This news is bitter in an old man's mouth—
	Elizabeth is murder'd?
Ernest	—So 'tis said.
	The messenger arriv'd to tell us so,
	Though never—even when my mother died,
	E'en when young William was too quickly ta'en, 5
	E'en when our poor Justine was doom'd to die,
	E'en when we heard of Henry's sudden death—
	Hath sorrow touch'd my heart as now it doth.
	Elizabeth was sinew, bones, and breath
	That kept our family alive through trial. 10
	Sans her, we have no star that guides us north,
	No compass wherewith our direction tell.
	Our family is curs'd; all else is false.
Alphonse	O, can it be—Elizabeth destroy'd?
Ernest	Thine aging mind doth work to shun the truth, 15
	Yet thou dost know it father: she is gone,
	Struck down with fingers 'round her lovely throat
	Like William and like Henry were before.
Alphonse	My charm and my delight, Elizabeth!
	My more than daughter, whom I doted on 20
	With all affection known to humankind,
	Who—as my life declines, with fewer ties
	To bind my spirit unto mortal matters—
	I clung to e'en more earnestly, in faith,

	O, is she dead?	
Ernest	—Yea, father, she is dead.	25
	Shalt thou be Peter, thus denying thrice?	
Alphonse	Thrice I'll be Peter in proclaiming love.	
	My sweetest, smartest lass—Elizabeth!	
Ernest	Dear father, there's yet more that thou must hear:	
	Our bravest visages we must display,	30
	For Victor shall return to us anon.	
Alphonse	If he come home not soon, 'tis probable	
	He shall find me a grave man, verily.	
	My heart doth tremble at these dismal tidings.	
Ernest	The messenger said Victor would arrive	35
	At any moment.	

[Alphonse moves to a couch.

Alphonse	—I must lie me down.	
	In answer to this new intelligence,	
	There's something breaks within me even now—	
	The clock that ticks within the human breast	
	Keeps time withal the beating of the heart,	40
	The gears and spinning wheels turn constantly	
	Within the case that doth contain the whole.	
	The face, the hands, the outward motions have	
	Vitality by complex inner workings.	
	There is some crucial spring come loose in me,	45
	Which slows the pendulum of Frankenstein.	
Ernest	Good sir, art well? Behold, thy son arrives!	

Enter VICTOR FRANKENSTEIN.

Victor	Home have I come with bearing humbl'd quite,	
	And what is this new tragedy I see—	
	Pray, Ernest, speak: how doth our father fare?	50
Ernest	Upon the instant he receiv'd the news	
	Of thine Elizabeth's demise most cruel,	
	He swoon'd and then betook himself to rest.	
Alphonse	Come hither, children, sit ye by my bed;	
	And hear, I think, the very latest counsel	55
	That ever I shall breathe.	
Victor	—Our ears are thine.	
Alphonse	I know not for what sin I am beset	
	By punishment divine and hellish torment.	
	Whate'er transgressions call me to account,	
	I do repent with deep, sincere remorse.	60
	Thus end the woes of Alphonse Frankenstein.	

[Alphonse dies.

Ernest	Our miseries do pile on one another	
	Like bricks that form a mausoleum's walls.	
	Farewell, wise father, founder of us all.	
Victor	[*aside:*] 'Tis mercy that he dies in his own time,	65
	Not claim'd by that foul fiend who hateth me.	
Ernest	I bid thee, Victor, to illuminate	
	The cause and circumstances of our grief.	
	I'd not lay blame before thy guiltless feet,	
	Yet death and murder seem to cling to thee	70

	Like crows that rush toward the carrion.	
	Thou—who, by illness, hast been sorely wrack'd,	
	And mir'd in melancholy constantly—	
	Art at the center of these agonies,	
	The common link within a chain of troubles.	75
Victor	Thy words are fitting, brother, and 'tis time	
	That I reveal the matter totally.	
	It is, indeed, a tale so strange that I	
	Should fear thou wouldst not credit it, were there	
	Not something in the truth, however doubtful,	80
	That forces its conviction on the mind.	
	Before I went to school at Ingolstadt,	
	I was already steep'd in fervent study	
	Of science, natural philosophy,	
	And all the wonders I could learn thereof.	85
Ernest	Well I recall the books thou carriedst e'er,	
	Of which our father oft was critical.	
Victor	'Tis true. These studies further I pursued	
	In Ingolstadt, when I matriculated.	
	Explaining the obsession wherewith I	90
	Was seiz'd is near impossible, I fear—	
	'Twas like the flicker of a flame inside,	
	And any effort to extinguish prov'd	
	But further fuel for the growing pyre.	
	Soon, I became convinc'd I had the pow'r—	95
	Giv'n only to the hands of deities—	
	To bring the dead to life, reanimate	
	Mere tissue and create a living being.	
Ernest	Preposterous and passing dangerous!	

Victor	True, brother. Yet my hubris led me on:	100
	I spent my time in charnel-houses rank,	
	To find the needed human parts for mine	
	Offensive and obscene experiments.	
Ernest	Nay, Victor!	
Victor	—Yet the strangest still shall come:	
	By fate or heav'n or hell—I know not what—	105
	I did succeed, and form'd a creature whose	
	Enormity match'd his deformity.	
	Would I had, thereupon, the brute destroy'd.	
	Instead, I fled in terror and dismay,	
	And chanc'd on Henry nearly instantly.	110
	From there, thou knowest what transpir'd with me.	
Ernest	'Twas when thou fellest ill for many months,	
	And then return'd when William murder'd was.	
Victor	Yea.	
Ernest	—Thinkest thou the beast hath done the deed?	
Victor	I think it not; I know it to be so.	115
Ernest	How canst thou, Victor?	
Victor	—I have seen the fiend,	
	Have spoken with him, heard it from his lips.	
Ernest	He speaks and hath confess'd his many crimes?	
Victor	Once I deserted him, he flew with haste	
	Toward the woods surrounding Ingolstadt.	120
	There, living in a hovel near a house,	

	He many months observ'd a family,	
	Absorbing language as he heard their words.	
Ernest	Remarkable! Belike the brain within	
	His rotting head had still the pow'r to learn.	125
Victor	E'en so. The monster did confess he slay'd	
	Poor William and entrapp'd our sad Justine.	
Ernest	The villain! That he still should walk the earth!	
Victor	There is yet more, which wholly painteth me	
	In darkest shades of culpability:	130
	The monster met me as I stroll'd upon	
	The mountains, after sweet Justine was hang'd.	
	He bid me undertake another chore,	
	Return unto the smelting furnace to	
	Create a female for his company.	135
Ernest	The brigand! Murderer and criminal,	
	To give an ultimatum such as this.	
	'Tis plain thou didst refuse.	
Victor	—Would that I had!	
	Yet 'twas not so, I timidly admit.	
	His argument, at first, seem'd justified,	140
	For I had giv'n him life, but ta'en away	
	All prospect of society for him	
	By making him abhorrent and deform'd.	
	Thus did I vow, the female to produce.	
Ernest	O, errant Victor. Didst thou do the deed?	145
	Is there a second creature who doth lurk	
	Around Geneva, plying murder's trade?	

Victor	Nay. As thou knowest, I to England went—
Ernest	A-ha! 'Tis why from Henry thou didst part.
	In Orkney wert thou at thy work again: 150
	Have I guess'd right?
Victor	—In details all but one:
	Once I bethought me of th'unknown effects
	Of making a companion for the brute,
	I stopp'd my work, wreck'd my laboratory.
Ernest	This, brother, was the only righteous choice. 155
Victor	Would it were so. But how, I cannot tell.
	The monster did observe mine ev'ry move,
	And on the instant I destroy'd my work
	Did he confront me with these haunting words:
	"I shall be with thee on thy wedding-night." 160
Ernest	Fie! Horror, horror past all reckoning.
	This, then, was thine Elizabeth's harsh fate.
Victor	Yea. Now hast thou hast heard ev'ry detail vile—
	Mine own invention hath undone me quite,
	Afflicting me with an eternal curse. 165
Ernest	What wilt thou do? The rogue still freely roams.
Victor	I do not doubt he hovers near the spot
	Which we inhabit even as we speak.
	If he hath taken refuge in the Alps,
	He may be hunted as a beast of prey. 170
Ernest	Haste! Let us call upon the magistrate,
	Who shall exert himself once he doth hear

	The story thou unfoldedst unto me.	
	If 'tis within his pow'r to seize the swine,	
	He thereupon shall suffer punishment	175
	Proportionate unto his hateful crimes.	
	I fear, though—from what thou hast told me of	
	His properties of power and deceit—	
	That snaring him shall prove unfeasible.	
	Belike we must prepare our grieving minds	180
	To know the prick of disappointment's jab.	
Victor	Nay, Ernest, nay, that cannot—shall not—be.	
	The swift revenge I seek is not thy task.	
	While I confess my vengeance is a vice,	
	'Tis the devouring passion of my soul,	185
	The fire that never shall be quench'd or dows'd.	
	Myself, whatever future days I have,	
	Shall be devoted to the fiend's destruction.	
Ernest	Canst thou not set aside this hatred and	
	Give others the responsibility?	190
Victor	Nay. Even as I did create the monster,	
	Which was the deep obsession I pursued,	
	Now must I undertake another chore,	
	Which I shall chase with equal appetite.	
	The monster's death must be my destiny,	195
	Which—till accomplish'd—burneth hot in me.	

[Exeunt.

SCENE 3.
The north.

Enter ROBERT WALTON.

Robert   If all the world is bound in our meek globe,
The theater of life play'd on a stage,
Then 'tis a moment aberrant when e'en
The Chorus doth become a player, too.
That moment most unnatural hath come,   5
When I—mere Chorus to this history—
Step forth as character within the tale.
'Twas as our ship press'd northward to the pole
And was fix'd fast within the icy floe,
That Frankenstein appearèd in the distance   10
And soon unveil'd for me his story grim.
Th'expression of his eyes was ever wild,
And oft was he a melancholy man,
Replete with such despair as hurt to see.
Should he be shown the smallest act of kindness,   15
His countenance would light like morning sun,
With sweetness of a starving man shown food.
'Twas gen'rally his wont, however, to
Appear so heavy 'neath the weight of woe
That all who look'd upon him pitied him.   20
Yea, thus was Victor Frankenstein to me,
When first I met him in the frozen wasteland.

Enter VICTOR FRANKENSTEIN.

Victor   Before I board your vessel, Captain Walton,
I prithee tell me whither you are bound.

Robert   Toward the north pole, there to claim our place   25
Within the hist'ry books as bold explorers.

Victor	'Tis well; in that direction am I led.	
Robert	What is your destination? And your sledge— Pull'd by a mangy, weak, exhausted mutt— Where can you hope to go, transported thus?	30
Victor	I seek the one who ever flees from me.	
Robert	This other person—were they so convey'd, In sledge most similar?	
Victor	—Indeed, he was.	
Robert	'Tis possible we spied him yesterday, For as we did attempt to break the ice, Some members of the crew declar'd they saw A figure riding on a dog-borne sleigh Far in the distance. We no more sign saw, And had dismiss'd the sight as fantasy.	35
Victor	The demon, then is near!	
Robert	—What demon, sir?	40
Victor	Sans doubt, your curiosity is piqu'd, As well as those of your crew members brave. Ye are too civil to make inquiry.	
Robert	'Twould be impertinent to trouble you By making inquisition needlessly.	45
Victor	Yet you have rescued me from peril, sir, For I was nearly dead upon the ice And you restore me unto health and life.	

Robert	Both harrowing and strange must be your tale,	
	And frightful was the storm that did embrace	50
	The vessel of your life and wreck it thus.	
Victor	'Tis far too late, my life or soul to save.	
	Yet mayhap shall my story work in you	
	Like blacksmith who doth work at forge and hammer,	
	To mold a better shape in cleansing fire.	55
	I sense in you a man much driven, like	
	Myself. And till my ghastly tale is told,	
	This heart within me burns.	
Robert	[*aside:*] —For many days,	
	As his own health and energy allow'd,	
	This Frankenstein his chronicle reveal'd.	60
	A kinship close to friendliness I felt	
	With this poor man, so mir'd in tragedy.	
	At last, he brought me to the present time.	
Victor	Departing from Geneva and good Ernest,	
	I follow'd that foul fiend as he fled north.	65
	My life, as it passed thus, did hateful grow,	
	And during sleep alone did I taste joy.	
	O blessed sleep, with dreams most rapturous!	
	The spirits that still guarded me did grant	
	These hours of happiness, my strength to bolster,	70
	That I might face my solemn pilgrimage.	
	Whilst it was day, I only wish'd for night,	
	For 'neath sleep's cloak I could, again, behold	
	My country, friends, and dear Elizabeth.	
	I saw my father's caring countenance,	75
	Heard silver tones—Elizabeth's pure voice—	
	And watch'd as Henry thriv'd in health and youth.	
	At times, I would find marks made by the monster—	

| | His childlike writing in the bark of trees, |
| | Or cut in stone upon my wretchèd path. 80
| | E'er did these signs my fury instigate.
| | One message I remember passing well:
| | "My reign is not yet over," writ the beast,
| | "Thou livest, and my power is complete.
| | Pursue me to the ices of the north, 85
| | Where thou shalt feel the ache of cold and frost,
| | To which I am impassive utterly.
| | Come hither, enemy: we are not done,
| | We've yet to wrestle for our very lives,
| | Like cunning Jacob and the blessèd angel, 90
| | Yet thou hast many miserable hours
| | Until that last encounter doth arrive."
| | These words rekindl'd ev'ry spark of hate—
| | Unto his death and torture I once more
| | Devoted what vitality I had. 95
| | Ne'er shall my search surcease until the day
| | When he or I do perish. Then, with joy,
| | I'll join Elizabeth and my lost friends,
| | Who now prepare the sacred recompense
| | For all my dreary toil and journeys dire. 100

Robert   This, then, is how thou camest hitherward?

Victor   Forsooth. The foe was nearly in my grasp
            When suddenly I lost all trace of him.
            Just then, the waters roll'd and swell'd beneath,
            More ominous and frightful with each breath, 105
            As if I'd given Neptune some offense.
            The wind arose, the sea roar'd horribly,
            And then an earthquake split the glacial ground.
            Upon a scatter'd piece of ice I drifted,
            Preparing for a slow and painful death. 110
            My dogs—the sole companions of my days—

	Each, one by one, succumb'd unto the cold.	
	'Twas then—as I prepar'd myself to die—	
	I saw thy vessel, proffering the hope	
	Of life and succor for the undeserving.	115

Robert Belike fate still hath purpose for thee yet.

Victor Yet, what of thee? I never knew a ship
To sail so deep within the northern climes,
And was astounded by the very sight.

Robert This voyage is the ardor of my soul. 120
I'd gladly sacrifice my fortune whole,
Forsake existence and mine ev'ry hope
An it would further this bold enterprise.
Troth, one man's life or death is a small price
To pay for all the knowledge I do seek, 125
For the dominion I should gain and hold
O'er ev'ry element.

Victor 　　　　　—Unhappy man!
Dost thou, too, share mine agonizing plight?
Hast also drunk th'intoxicating draught
Of lunacy? Art thou, like me, aflame 130
With that Promethean heat that never dies?
Thou still hast hope—the world before thee lies—
With no despair to shake thee at thy core,
Whilst I've lost ev'rything once dear to me,
And never can reset my little life. 135
Thou hast my story heard in ev'ry jot.
Once had I thought its memory should die
With me, but thou hast alter'd my resolve.
Thou seekest knowledge and her sister, wisdom,
As once I did, and 'tis mine earnest hope 140
The satisfaction of thy fervent wish

	Becometh not a serpent that doth sting,
	As mine hath been. Pursuing that same course
	That once I ran, thou dost expose thyself
	Unto the selfsame dangers I have fac'd. 145
	I beg thee, find a moral in my tale,
	Which may direct thy steps this moment forward.
	Create not for thyself an enemy
	Demonical—instead, learn from my grief,
	And seek thou not thine own woes to increase. 150

Robert   Thine utt'rance, Victor, shakes me heartily.
           I'll think upon thy words, I promise thee.

Victor   Do. Save thyself ere thou becomest me—
           Too rent by woe and vengeance to be free.
           The only joy that I can ever know   155
           Is when my shatter'd spirit is releas'd
           To peace and death.

Robert   —Must I, then, be bereft?
           Long have I sought for such a friend as thou.
           Upon the desert seas did I find thee—
           Shall I thy value know and lose thee, then?   160

Victor   I thank thee, Walton, for thy kind intentions
           Unto a wretch as desolate as I.
           Yet, when thou speakest of affections new,
           Think'st any can replace those who are gone?
           Can any be to me as Henry was,   165
           Another woman be Elizabeth?
           They both are dead, and for one purpose only
           Am I persuaded to preserve my life.
           I must destroy the being unto whom
           I gave existence; then my lot on earth   170
           Shall be fulfilled and I may die at last.

Enter two CREW MEMBERS.

Crew 1	[*to Robert:*] Pray, Captain, we must speak to you alone.
Robert	Speak freely. I shall not fear this man's trust.
Crew 2	The crew have gather'd and discuss'd at length Our present situation in the ice.　　　　　　175 Withal united voice, we do implore: If, by the gods, the ice doth dissipate, And we some passage open through the floe, We beg thee, on the instant, to turn south.
Crew 1	We've no more hope, the north pole to attain.　180 The flames that once did blaze without our souls Are snuff'd in cold and ice and endless toil.
Robert	[*aside:*] Alas, can I refuse this just demand? 'Tis terrible to think the lives of all These people are endanger'd by my will.　　　185 If we are lost, my mad schemes are the cause. Still, I had rather die than flee in shame, Returning home with purpose unfulfill'd.

　　　　　　　　　　　　　　　　　　　[Victor collapses.

Crew 2	Behold, the castaway doth swoon.
Crew 1	—He falls!
Robert	Say, Victor, art thou well? Pray, comrade, speak!　190
Victor	Alack, the strength on which I have relied Is gone, and death is knocking at my door.

          My enemy and persecutor lives—
          That he should live to be an instrument
          Of mischief doth disturb me in the height.   195
          Still, though, this hour—as I expect release—
          Is th'only happy one I have enjoy'd
          These many mournful years. The forms of my
          Belovèd dead do flit before mine eyes,
          And gladly shall I hasten to their arms.   200
          Peace be thine, Walton! Seek thou happiness
          And shun ambition, which to ashes leads.
          What, should I stay—

                                                    [*Victor dies.*

Robert   —In this vile world? Farewell.
          Now boast thee, death, in thy possession lies
          A man unparallel'd.

                    Enter CREW MEMBER 3.

Crew 3   —O Captain, hear!   205
          A specter horrible approacheth us,
          In form much like a man, yet so deform'd
          And so immense as could not human be.

Robert   It is the monster, come to meet his maker!
          Make signs of peace and show him to my door.   210

Crew 3   E'en as you say, sir, though to look on him
          Hath frighted me past any aspect of
          Our misadventure in the mighty north.

                                            [*Exit crew member 3.*

Robert	[*to crew 1 and 2:*] Good gentles, stand you guard whilst we two speak.	
	The visitor may yet prove dangerous,	215
	Though little reason hath for harming me.	
Crew 2	We shall, sir. Pray, remember what we ask'd.	
Robert	I'll think upon the theme of your request,	
	And give an answer to your suit anon.	

Enter THE MONSTER with CREW MEMBER 3.

Monster	Another victim claim'd! His murder is	220
	The consummation of my many crimes,	
	The dread tasks of my life come to a close.	
	O, Frankenstein! Kind, self-devoted being!	
	My rage is gone, and I am struck with sorrow.	
	What worth is it to ask thee for thy pardon,	225
	Who thee destroy'd and all thou ever lov'dst?	
	Alas! He's cold, and never shall respond,	
	Yet he shall have a noble memory.	
Robert	[*aside:*] Such passion and contrition unforeseen.	
	[*To monster:*] Your late repentance is superfluous.	230
	Had you but listen'd to the voice of conscience,	
	And heeded inner stirrings of remorse	
	Ere you urg'd vengeance to the breaking point,	
	Your Victor Frankenstein would yet have liv'd.	
Monster	Do you dream I am dead to agony,	235
	Or stranger to remorse? Do you believe	
	The groans of Clerval were an anthem sweet?	
	Nay, he did fashion me withal a heart	
	Susceptible to love and sympathy.	
	When wrench'd by misery to vice and hate,	240

                    The torture was beyond imagining.
                    Yet still, whilst piling wretchedness on me,
                    My maker dar'd to hope for happiness—
                    He sought enjoyment in the very feelings
                    From which I was, by him, forever barr'd.   245
                    He fin'lly promis'd me companionship,
                    But chang'd his mind and stole my future bliss.
                    This spurr'd my taste for vengeance, and 'twas then
                    I took my payment from his young bride's neck.
                    My work is done; there my last victim lies.   250

Robert   Ha! Do you come to whine o'er all the woes
                    That were accomplish'd at your willing hand?
                    You throw a torch into a building's frame,
                    And when it is consum'd, you do lament.
                    O fiend most hypocritical indeed!   255
                    If he whom you do mourn were still alive,
                    Still would he be the object and the prey
                    Of your accursèd vengeance, would he not?
                    'Tis not compassion you are feeling, sirrah:
                    You are but disappointed that the aim   260
                    Of thy transgressions is beyond your pow'r.

Monster   Nay, 'tis not thus, despite what I do seem.
                    I seek no fellow feeling in my grief;
                    No sympathy, belike, I'll ever find.
                    I am content to suffer this alone,   265
                    And when I die I shall abhorrèd be
                    Within the memories of all I touch'd.
                    Once had I dreams of virtue, fame, and joy,
                    Once falsely wish'd I would a being find
                    Who would my rank appearance pardon and   270
                    Love me for many other qualities.
                    My crimes, though, have degraded me beneath
                    The meanest and most savage animal.

No guilt or mischief doth compare with mine,
The fallen angel turns malignant devil. 275
You seem to have deep knowledge of my crimes—
Why hate not Felix, who did drive me out?
Why hate not William, who but scream'd at me?
Why hate not Victor, who deserted me?
'Tis certain, though, I am a horrid beast, 280
Who murder'd lovely, helpless innocents.
Mine own creator I pursued to ruin,
And there he lieth, white and cold in death.
You hate me, yea, but your abhorrence ne'er
Can equal that with which I view myself. 285
I look upon the hands that did the deed,
I think upon the heart that did conceive 't,
And long for when I'll no more haunted be
By hands or heart, or harsh imagination.

Robert You have your answer, there your maker lies. 290
What shall you do with those who do remain?
What move is next, now you have ta'en the pawns
And played your checkmate on the noble king?

Monster My work is near complete. I'll quit your ship,
And seek the northernmost extremities 295
Of this, our globe, upon mine ice raft small.
There, mine own pyre I gladly shall collect,
And let this frame to ashes be return'd,
That its remains may not afford a light
To some mind curious, which would create 300
Another dreadful being like myself.
I shall no longer feel the agonies
That now consume me, 'tis a consummation
Devoutly to be wish'd. To death I'll go—
Light, feeling, and all sense shall pass away, 305
And in that moment I'll find happiness.

Robert	Must it be thus? For yea, despite your crimes,
	Some marks of charity I spy in you,
	The possibility of penitence.
Monster	Nay, soon these burning griefs shall be extinct. 310
	Farewell, you last of humankind I'll see,
	Farewell, dear man who made me and unmade me.

[Exit monster in haste.

Robert	Pursue him, let him not escape!
Crew 3	—We shall!

[Exeunt crew members. Robert Walton addresses the audience, as Epilogue.

Robert	He ne'er was found, amid the frost and ice,
	And we laid Victor in a wat'ry grave. 315
	Perchance the monster did persist in vice,
	Perchance, in fire, he died his soul to save.
	Yet I did learn the lesson of their tale;
	Home seem'd more precious far than wealth or fame,
	And, thus, toward the south did we set sail. 320
	Let other parties smolder in the flame,
	Let other captains strive to claim the pole—
	Our path was homeward set, our fervor snuff'd.
	We few would not, like Victor, pay the toll
	Each person pays when virtue is rebuff'd. 325
	Extinguish'd is the fire that burn'd within.
	Now: homeward fly, our new lives to begin.

[Exeunt omnes.

AFTERWORD

In early September 2020—after six months of coronavirus isolation and daily protests against injustice on our streets—wildfires came to Oregon. My home, in Portland, was safe from the fires, but the apocalyptic yellow-gray sky, with the refuge of going outside taken away from us, made the situation feel even more hopeless than it had before.

It was in that atmosphere (literally) that I decided to write and freely distribute a Shakespearean adaptation of a classic horror tale, in time for Halloween. For a few years, I've been thinking about writing adaptations of Mary Shelley's *Frankenstein*, Robert Louis Stevenson's *Strange Case of Dr. Jekyll and Mr. Hyde*, and Bram Stoker's *Dracula*. I asked Twitter which one I should write, and here we are.

This is one of the fastest adaptations I've ever written, and it was fun to share my daily process on Twitter as I wrote the book and distributed it as a weekly serial throughout October. People who know my other books will know that there are Shakespearean references and Easter eggs dotted throughout the book (including three acrostics—you'll find them). The text is about half adapted directly from Shelley and half my own invention for the purpose of plot, character, or sense.

In case you're wondering about the scene at the start of Act IV, Scene 1, between the two Orkney villagers: I spent three months living in the Orkney islands with my family in 2014—*William Shakespeare's The Clone Army Attacketh* was written there—and I have a deep affection for the islands. (Don't be surprised if I'm living there in a few years!) When I read *Frankenstein*, I was delighted to discover that part of the story takes place in Orkney, and I quickly decided to write a brief scene that highlighted the islands and its people. Mary Shelley is not complimentary about Orkney:

> It was a place fitted for such a work, being hardly more than a rock whose high sides were continually beaten upon by the waves. The soil was barren, scarcely affording pasture for a few miserable cows, and oatmeal for its inhabitants, which consisted of five persons, whose gaunt and scraggy limbs gave tokens of their miserable fare.

The truth is that the Orkney Islands are wonderful. Hence this scene, which features the names of my dear friends in Orkney, Helga and

Michael, and borrows many words from Orkney's unique dialect. Many thanks to orkneydictionary.scot for vocabulary help.

Thank you to everyone who voted in the Twitter poll when I was deciding which book to write and encouraged me along the way—I'll get to *Strange Case of Dr. Jekyll and Mr. Hyde* and *Dracula* sometime, I promise. Thank you to Michael Bolan, who suggested a Doctor Faustus-inspired title for the book. Thank you to my colleagues at Quirk Books, who support me even when I'm going off the traditional publishing path. Thank you to Nicole De Jackmo, from Quirk, who suggested releasing the book as a serial. Thank you to the creative team, actors, and groundings of The Show Must Go Online, my favorite artistic endeavor to come out of the COVID-19 pandemic. Thank you to Jennifer, Liam, Graham, and Joseph, whose love makes everything possible.

This book was born out of the wildfires in Oregon, which is fitting since fire is one of the themes of *Frankenstein* (its subtitle is, of course, "The Modern Prometheus"). My adaptation's cover, the opening Chorus monologue, and many other moments throughout the book suggest that something is burning, and that something may well be us. Here's hoping the fire within us will burn not in misdirected passion—as Victor's did—but for justice, for creativity, and for good.

—October 30, 2020
Portland, Oregon

Ian Doescher is the *New York Times* bestselling author of the *William Shakespeare Star Wars* series, the Pop Shakespeare series, and other books. He lives in Portland, Oregon with his spouse Jennifer, teenagers Liam and Graham, and dog Thorfinn. Find Ian online at iandoescher.com.

CPSIA information can be obtained
at www.ICGtesting.com
Printed in the USA
LVHW081744290522
720038LV00007B/303